To Christine,

With best wishes
from,
Gina

About the Author

Georgina Evans is the author of this her first novel. She is married and she lives on the Shropshire/Welsh borders.

She has written plays, sketches and a pantomime for her local amateur dramatic society.

She has worked in business and further education and qualified as a teacher in 2011.

Georgina has a passion for equality and diversity issues and has worked in this capacity within a large college.

She enjoys art and listening to an eclectic range of music but Mozart is undoubtedly her favourite composer.

Dedication

In memory of Paula Brown who encouraged and inspired me to start writing and to my loving husband Andrew for his faith and support.

Georgina Evans

SLEEPING WITH AMADEUS

AUSTIN MACAULEY
PUBLISHERS LTD.

A CIP catalogue record for this title is available from the British Library.

ISBN 978 1 78455 383 8 (Paperback)
ISBN 978 1 78455 385 2 (Hardback)

www.austinmacauley.com

First Published (2015)
Austin Macauley Publishers Ltd.
25 Canada Square
Canary Wharf
London
E14 5LB

Printed and bound in Great Britain

Acknowledgments

Bach, Chopin and Mozart, thank you.

Chapter 1

The flat was bare and green mould grew wild like filigree across the blackened windows. A toddler walked about on the hard tiles, bending down occasionally to scrub at the floor and examine debris, wondering whether to eat it. Her dark eyes scoured the dark room, searching for her mother. An empty bottle dangled from her blue tinted mouth, the curdled milk clinging to the sides as it bobbed along in time to her gait. Her feet were bruised and cut, her face scratched and blotchy. Her lonely little body teetered forwards, falling across her mother's form lying still in the dark; yet warm, so warm.

The child made a noise. Not a cry but a whimper. Her little lungs struggled to make a sound as she nestled into the arc of her curled parent beside her. She pulled at her mother's cardigan, wrapping it across her legs. Soon she slept; just there.

When she awoke there was a dim light and the cold crept back into her tiny frame. She felt pain and her bones creaked as she rubbed her sticky eyes and adjusted to the light of the room. She saw her mother at the doorway, a shard of light passing through her cloudy skirt.

"Can you lend me some money? I needs it to feed the baby" her mother said.

On the landing, Magdalene stopped her busy footsteps cloaked in smart patent leather court shoes and turned to the voice coming from the crack of the door. She wore her hair in a neat French wrap, her clean white blouse and her tight suit hugged her curvaceous bosom and hips. She had painted her nails red, matched by pouting red lips, and she opened them with surprise.

"Sorry, what did you say?"

The mother stared at her, her deep brown eyes glazed with nothing behind them.

"Can you lend me some money? I need to feed the baby. I get me social next Wednesday. I'll pay you back then."

Magdalene drew nearer. She was familiar with the girl across the landing. She had seen her dishevelled, her piercings and tattoos and had been able to smell her unwashed body. She had ignored the frequency of dodgy looking men arriving at her door with their long unkempt hair and the same unwashed smell. That smell lingered in the blank sterile landing area and Magdalene sometimes smelled it on her own clothes. Imagined or otherwise, she would sometimes strip off and put her things in the washing machine. It wasn't just dirt; it was urine, blood and sex. It was wisps of those smells creeping through the door as she looked upon the vivid girl, her dull eyes staring back with a blank faraway look that seeped into Magdalene's nostrils.

"Baby? I didn't know that you had a baby?" Magdalene said.

Perhaps it was fate or some strange coincidence but just at that moment the toddler pulled herself up and staggered like a drunk towards the door. Perhaps it was the light that drew her there. It was at that moment that Magdalene first set her own brown eyes on the little child. She was horrified by what she saw.

Inside Magdalene's head her brain seemed to scream. It flitted backwards and forwards, but the chain reaction that occurred in her thoughts in those few seconds would change the little girl's and her own life forever. "*Think, think*" her thoughts were saying, becoming calmer now, softer and ordered.

"Ah, hmm, money," she said. "For your baby?" She was focused on the child, the poor dear little child. The mother had not noticed her gaze or even the child beside her. She became agitated.

"Yeah, money for the baby innit!" she spoke violently.

Magdalene stood her ground.

"Well, I have a very important appointment this morning but I could drop some money by later after work?"

"Whatever," said the mother and began to close the door.

Magdalene felt giddy, her stomach was heaving, her mind was racing but she knew, she knew what she was going to do.

Opening her smart, oversized handbag, Magdalene took out her purse and offered the girl a twenty pound note.

"That's all I have right now," she said thrusting it at the crack in the door. "Here, please take it. I'll bring you some more very soon."

A grubby hand snatched the note from her grasp and shut the door. As she turned the child wobbled, fell and banged her head hard on the floor. The mother did not notice as she shrugged on her cardigan, pulled on black studded boots. Shutting the door behind her, she went to meet her dealer.

Magdalene had jogged down the three flights of stairs, her ample bosom rising and falling, a few brown hairs escaping, sneaking out deftly from the strong but fashionable knitted clip. She was perspiring as she dashed away from the smell of piss, blood and human waste and with an innate determination headed for the Tube station knowing exactly what she needed to do.

Her body swished and collided with other passengers as she gathered momentum, heading towards the waiting interview panel and the life-changing interview.

After the interview, she wanted to go for a coffee or a glass of wine to help calm her nerves; the anxious adrenaline was still surging through her body, catching in her throat. Despite this she was sure it had gone well. She tried hard to recall what the questions were, how had she replied and what she had said when they asked if she had any questions of her own. In truth she had forgotten. The only thing consuming her mind was that neglected child waiting for her. Something new was surging up inside her; she did not recognise it, but she liked this feeling. Was it power? Karma, maybe? She headed back to the Tube but decided to call in at a little bistro and ordered a large glass of red wine. Her head was spinning, her mind was full of a replay of her interview, searching inside to visualise their faces, their smiles, those people who held her future in their hands. Little did they know how important their decision was. Life-changing? No, she thought, it was about changing the fate of not just one but three people now, how powerful but unknowing that panel were.

As she sipped the gorgeous wine that cooled and calmed her, Magdalene thought about how her life had changed in the last year. For her, everything was turning, like the world rotating on its axis, her life was sometimes in the dark but lately - and she hoped this would always be - her destiny was moving with ease into the sunshine.

Chapter 2

That evening when she opened the door to her flat she glanced over towards where the drugged girl and her baby lived.

"Hang on little sweet child, hang on. I'm going to save you. I'm going to love you. Please just hang on a little longer," she whispered.

She wavered and wondered what would happen if she knocked on the grey filthy door, but she heard a noise from the stairs. Two large black men, dreadlocks swaying, came up to the landing where she stood. One of them smiled at her, his white teeth straight, his face beautiful. She watched but they did not go to the grey door, they continued along the landing and made a rat-a-tat-tat at the door on the end. Magdalene heard squeals of delight as someone, who appeared to be their mother, snatched them into a glow of warmth and she could hear laughter and chatter as the door shut behind them. *It's funny what goes on behind closed doors,* she thought. *No one ever knows what roles are played out, how dreams are made or how those dreams expire. Who loves and who dies and who, if anyone, is left behind.*

No one will ever know what I am going to say and do when I step inside my home and seal the entrance to another world. For in my own world, for what it is now and God willing, for what it is going to become. Magdalene had a feeling of overwhelming fatalism and that within her unconscious mind there was a mechanism driving uncontrollable thoughts about the child that she knew she could not stop.

"Hi honey," Lisa said. "How did it go? Okay? You must be shattered. Come on, I've opened some wine, let's have a glass and you can tell me all about it."

Lisa opened the bottle in the tiny kitchen inside their London flat. Her long fingers wrapped deftly around the bottle as she poured.

"Here, you'll need this," she said.

Magdalene listened to the glug, glug of the wine as it fell like a waterfall into the crystal goblet. The allure of the gushing red liquid fixed upon her as a strange feeling of blood falling through the air.

Lisa noticed that Magdalene was distant. *Probably because of the stress,* she thought. So much was hanging on that interview. If Magdalene got the job they could leave London, go to the countryside; she had heard Kent was lovely. Make a fresh start. What a cliché, but it was true. A fresh start.

Magdalene moved to the lounge and took off her shoes. She rubbed her feet, sore and swollen from the long day.

"Here, I'll do that," Lisa said.

She kneeled and took Magdalene's feet, massaging them gently, pulling at her toes.

The telephone rang.

Magdalene looked at Lisa, who stopped rubbing and she stared back at her.

"Oh my God," she said. "This is it!"

Lisa listened intently as Magdalene breathed heavily, her voice trembled and her legs and hands shook a little. She smiled. Lisa knew from the way the conversation was going that Magdalene had got the job and she could not wait for her to put the phone down. When she did they both cried for joy and they hugged and kissed and drank the wine and then opened another bottle and drank that too.

At about two in the morning, Magdalene sat up on the sofa where she had been laying, stroking Lisa's long blonde hair.

"There's something else," she said.

Lisa sat up with a jolt.

"You're not going to leave me are you?" she said, her blue eyes wide. Lisa cried, her voice faltering. "Oh no, have you found someone else?"

"Not someone else, you daft bat," Magdalene said. "How you tune those pianos with those ears I'll never know," she laughed. "Something else, something else," she repeated, to make sure Lisa was listening.

"We're going to have a baby!" Magdalene knew it sounded like an announcement. She realised as the words came out that she sounded like a heterosexual woman announcing to her male partner that after all those years of trying, they had succeeded, they were going to have a baby. She had longed for a baby with her husband but he had kept putting it off with the reasoning that they needed to build up their finances before taking the step of parenthood. Magdalene often wondered if that was the truth, that if they had cut down on a few things they could easily have managed for her to give up work for a while. She put it down to his selfishness and habits. A baby would just get in his way, is what she had concluded.

Lisa was catapulted out of her boozy slumber.

"Did you say that we are going to have a baby?" Lisa was unsure that she had heard Magdalene right. She was half asleep and her mind was just getting to grips with the fact that Magdalene wasn't going to leave her.

"Well, not exactly a baby. A toddler, a little girl. She's so cute, well, she's not cute at this point in time but she can be, she will be." Magdalene was talking quickly and Lisa was confused.

"Ok, listen, I've got something to tell you."

Magdalene told Lisa about the little child across the landing with the drugged-up mother. She explained that it was like an epiphany, she knew that God or something had meant for her to be there, on the landing, at that moment when the child appeared.

"You should see her, Leese." Magdalene felt tears welling in her eyes and she let go a long tearful sob. Her shoulders heaved and Lisa put her arms around her and held her tight.

Lisa felt her tummy churn as if she was riding a roller-coaster. Everything had moved so fast between her and Magdalene and now they were going to become parents. No, worse! Abductors! However, she loved Magdalene, she was clever and her Irish lilt could soothe Lisa into any decision, and Lisa trusted her implicitly. She genuinely felt moved when Magdalene told her of the little girl across the landing. Lisa knew from empirical experience how easy it was for neglect to seep into the lives of children that were unwanted and unloved by their parents. She recalled the recent news about a small boy who had been surrounded by a huge number of multi-agency workers, who had died in the care of his own mother and stepfather. Maybe Mags was right, and this was an opportunity to give the little child a new life. Without more thought, and waving away any creeping doubts, she agreed with Magdalene on her plans for the poor little girl.

Soon, everything was in action. Whilst Magdalene worked out her notice, Lisa spent her days between her clients and arranging removal men, not that they had much to move but they both liked the thought of their minimal belongings arriving in style. Anyway, as part of their plan, it had become essential now that Lisa had arrived with the removal van.

Lisa had found the black and white cottage in a sweet Kent village. A long path led to a rose border sculpted in front of two small windows that lay either side of the black old oak front door. Honeysuckle interfered with the orderly roses growing patterns which clung tenaciously to the brittle porch cover. The smells were heavenly, not a whiff of urine or sick or blood or sweat. Tracing the path revealed French lavender, dahlias, stock and more perfumed roses. The houses around were bountiful in their horticulture, Georgian sash windows and neatly cut lawns. Both women fell in love with the cottage, the village, the village pub, the long walks and the tea room on their frequent visits to their own Eden.

The day came.

Lisa busied herself with the removal men, constantly apologising that the lift didn't work and making huge mugs of tea and offering plates of biscuits. It only took an hour to take their belongings down to the van. Lisa sat in the cab with the men who flirted with her and teased her and begged for her to make more tea at the other end. She joined in with their chatter, she felt brave as she watched the scenes of London fade away to a sunlit haze, golden fields, sheep grazing, cows chewing the cud, forming a pre-cursor point in her mind and heart towards paradise.

During the journey she reflected on how she had felt shocked when Magdalene had told her about her plan to take the little girl, and the poor health and state of the child. Growing up she had come across children similar to those of the child across the hall. She felt huge empathy. Now she felt pleased that she went along with Magdalene's proposals to rescue a child from a future that would be filled with dread and terror. In many ways Magdalene's plan made her feel more secure, as having a child was a permanent step and would bind the two women in their love forever. She was praying that all was going well for Magdalene. She turned and gave the driver a huge smile.

"Nearly there," she said.

Magdalene picked up the hire car. She had packed a large holdall with a blanket, a baby's bottle, some milk and rusks, jars of baby food, disposable nappies, baby wipes, a baby's night time sleeping bag and a pack of six pink all-in-one toddler suits. It was summer and Magdalene wore white cotton cut-offs with a flowing white lilac cotton shirt and pink pumps. Her unruly hair, dark and curly, was swept up in a casual ponytail. Her freckles gave her the air of a child and on this day Magdalene carried herself along with the face of an angel.

Thanking the car hire salesman and explaining that even though, yes, it was a hot summer's day, she would prefer to drive through London with the hood down, she drove away knowing that it wasn't because of the smog, of course, it was because she wanted to keep her little parcel out of sight.

Magdalene called at the cash point and took out £500. Her heart was thumping so she turned up the radio to block out the sounds of the voice inside her head. Was there any doubt in there? No, she was sure that there wasn't. All she could hope for now was that the drug girl would open the door. Would she let her in?

Magdalene parked the car in a white-lined bay outside the block of flats. She wouldn't have long before the car attracted the attention of local car vandals and thieves. She would have to be quick.

She raced up the two flights of stairs. It was ten o'clock on a Saturday so most people would still be sleeping off the ill effects of the night before. There was the door to her flat. All was quiet. Lisa had gone in the van with her old life fading through London streets, the crowds and the city falling away, disappearing from her soul like a spell. She thought about checking inside their flat, just to make sure that Lisa had taken everything but she knew there would be no time.

Double checking that no one was about, she nervously tapped on the grey door. She was afraid to knock too loudly as she didn't want anyone else to hear. It was fruitless, of course, as no one answered. She tapped again, louder, then again, louder. She was tempted to look through the letter box and was just about to when a crack appeared in the door.

The girl looked puzzled at the woman standing there. At first she thought Magdalene might be a social worker but there was some faint recognition, so she just stayed there staring, half asleep, yawning, scratching at her needle points on her long thin tattooed arm.

"Hello," Magdalene said. "You might not remember but I loaned you £20 a while ago? Oh no, don't worry, I don't want it back. I've brought you some more money, look." Magdalene took out the wad of cash from her pocket.

"It's for you, so that you can buy food for your little girl and yourself, naturally," she said handing out the cash to the girl. It was as if the cash was a piece of meat that she was giving to a lion, as she felt afraid, afraid that this girl with vacant eyes would suss her out and eat her.

The girl reached out to take it. Magdalene steeled herself and said,

"Urm, I wondered whether you would like me to look after your baby, erm, little girl, while you went food shopping? It's a beautiful day and I could take her to the park, it's no trouble, really."

The girl shut the door. Magdalene stood, breathless. Would it open again? In her head she prayed. She didn't know what to do, her mind was racing but she stood there as still as a statue. A few minutes later the door opened and the girl held the child in her arms. The child was floppy; her deep brown eyes ringed with dark circles and Magdalene had that strange feeling again. Was this pity? Was it love? It was powerful but it wasn't power. The girl handed over the lifeless bundle and snatched the money from Magdalene's hand.

"Don't know 'ow long I'm gonna be," said the girl, her stinking breath showering Magdalene as she spoke.

"That's fine," said Magdalene. "Please, be as long as you like, I'll return her later, much later so that you can get on with your errands and buy some food." She sounded pompous, like an old school mistress but it was too late to change her tone as the girl shut the door hard in her face.

She walked steadily down the stairs fearing that she would drop the child or that someone would put a hand on her shoulder and ask her where she was going or question what she was doing.

When she got to the car and saw that it was still intact she sighed with relief. It was only a two-door and it was a struggle to open the passenger side and put the seat down whilst holding onto her rag doll who she laid on the back seat. She had thought about hiring a car seat but she could not very well

21

hide a little girl's body if she was sitting up. The child didn't move, nor did she make a sound. Magdalene stroked her hair.

"Hang on, little one. Leese and I will love you. We will take care of you. Hang on, not long now..."

As Magdalene drove slowly away from the estate she could not help looking into her rear view mirror. Surely the mother would come? Magdalene imagined her running after them, her fragile hair and tasteless tattoos and piercings glinting in the sunlight as her thin legs gained ground on them as she cursed Magdalene with her vile breath and muddied teeth.

To her relief, no one noticed her, no one chased them and soon the streets of London were left behind as the child slept and teetered between starvation and life in the back of a hire car with a stranger, a woman who in an instant had changed her life forever.

Lisa had finally managed to get rid of the removal men and had begun to make up the cot in the small bedroom at the back of the upstairs floor in the cottage. She did this with confidence, she knew Mags would do it, nothing ever deterred her. Hadn't she walked out of that comfortable marriage, shocking her husband, family and the catholic priest, a life-long friend of her family, when she declared that she was in love with someone else? And that someone else happened to be a woman!

Lisa had never met Mags' husband but she thought that she spied him once coming out of the courtroom after the divorce. He was handsome, very Irish looking with a kind freckled face and blue eyes, curtained with lush black hair. Magdalene had lost touch with everyone, or rather, they had lost touch with her, a shamed husband and family who were not equipped to come to terms with a 'fallen woman' as they had put it, which Lisa rather thought compared Magdalene to a prostitute.

Neither woman had discussed how anyone else involved in their actions must have felt. Those emotions would create a void between them and they made a vow to each other that they would live out their lives like the 'Ladies of Llangollen', attached to one another, not caring what the world thought of them. It was easy for Lisa and Magdalene, they had no friends. Lisa came from an orphanage and had come by accident to find her talents as a musician and piano tuner. As a child she played compact discs in her bedroom. This was her luxury away from the other kids who teased her about her gangly legs and buck teeth. Just like a revengeful fairy tale she had blossomed as she grew into a tall, slim and beautiful woman. But this had only made the other girls at the orphanage jealous who bullied her, and she became withdrawn.

One of the carers played the piano and sang. It took Lisa six months to pluck up the courage to shyly stand next to the carer, watching her hands play up and down over the keyboard. The carer was kind and intrigued by the pretty girl beside her. Her name was Ann and she was probably only five years older than Lisa but she had a maturity that shone through and she soon encouraged Lisa to sit and play, teaching her the basics. Quickly, Ann realised that Lisa had a talent and as Lisa's confidence grew, she was given piano lessons, then violin lessons, and then she did not need any more lessons because she mastered them both and passed her musical grades expediently.

She was daydreaming about how she and Magdalene had met, that first time when she had gone to her upmarket house in Hampstead to tune the old baby-grand piano. She recalled Magdalene's wicked smile and her straight even teeth. She had offered Lisa tea, or perhaps some wine in the garden?

They got along, these two young women with their different backgrounds, their different ambitions and dreams, but a strange connection was drawing them closer. Each felt it but never raised the point except once when they each agreed that despite being strangers, the couple had so much in common. They both liked to travel (although Lisa admitted that she had never travelled anywhere, but that she had ambitions to do so). They liked the same music and shared a love of opera. Magdalene introduced Lisa to Irish folk music and she played the guitar and sang old Irish love songs to Lisa in the garden with twinkling eyes that smiled as she vocalised tunes of loss and desire.

Lisa had absorbed Magdalene, letting her seep through her skin. She caught wisps of her scent as she freely responded to her many questions. Magdalene was curious about her young piano tuner. She told Lisa that she used to have a blind man to come and tune the piano but he had died unexpectedly from a heart attack. She had seen Lisa's advertisement in the local newsagent and was surprised when this long-legged girl with shiny blonde hair turned up.

"Not quite what I was expecting," Magdalene had said. "You know, in my mind's eye I thought you were likely going to be wearing a twin set, sensible shoes and pearls!" As she spoke she studied the girl before her, her slim waist, her glasses perched on her nose. Were her eyes blue or green? Most of all she admired her slender fingers. "Musician's fingers," Magdalene thought to herself, comparing them to her own small chubby ones.

Every time Lisa visited she became adept at dragging out conversations with Magdalene. She enjoyed her company so much and the way her light and relaxed way of engaging her made her feel, so much that she felt she would tell her anything she ever wanted to know about her. Secrets.

In those times she yearned for Magdalene to love her, desire her and she imagined them together making love, laughing and drinking wine, which she had become quite fond of owing to her frequent visits to Magdalene's home. She had no idea how Magdalene felt but somehow deep down she felt that Magdalene was fighting her feelings. All Lisa could do was to continue her visits and close her eyes and dream.

One day in the garden, Magdalene kissed her full on her lips, her moist mouth tasting of Merlot. Lisa responded, surprised but soaking in the moment. Lisa nervously reached out her hand to touch Magdalene's curls, kissing her neck. Then, reaching for her breasts beneath her cotton blouse, she undid the buttons. She caressed the warm fleshy skin which felt rounded and firm. She found a mole beside her nipple and playfully bent down to kiss it, teasing with her mouth and tongue, touching, touching and reaching out around the curves and crevices of her desire. Lifting her head she gazed into Magdalene's brown eyes, falling in love, in love with her, her body, her sex. They aroused and pleasured each other, right there in the garden. Afterwards, there was no embarrassing silence as they dressed and stroked each other's hair; there were only whispers and sighs.

"Visit tomorrow, please?" Magdalene had said, and Lisa nodded. She picked up her bag and left, knowing in that moment she was soaring with happiness, joy and love. As she looked back, Magdalene was watching her and blew her a kiss. Lisa laughed and blew Magdalene a kiss back.

Soon the piano was no longer needed as an excuse for Lisa to visit, and she and Magdalene often made love in the same bed that Magdalene shared with her husband. Neither of them had felt guilty. It had just felt right, and they would spend long days talking on the bed, flirting and fondling each other. Soon they were talking about being together, and how could this be?

That day arrived, planned, swift and decisive. Together they had faced many pitfalls incurred by the wrath of Magdalene's husband and family but they had come through. Now, this day had come too and they would face what was to come in the future together.

Chapter 3

Lisa heard the car on the gravel and ran down the stairs to open the door, to greet her love and their little girl, who was to be born of them and loved by them.

Magdalene carried the blanket into the house, hoping that if anyone was watching they would think that it was a cat or a precious inanimate object swaddled for its protection. She laid it down on the large cushioned sofa that was too big for the room but was deep and soft and cosy. She unwrapped the blanket revealing a thin dirty doll and Lisa whimpered, the shock was too much. She had not anticipated the appalling state of the child and her body reacted. She ran to the kitchen and retched but no fluid came out, just an agonising cry. She flushed cold water over her face and composed herself.

"Lisa, is there any hot water? Can you bring in a bowl of warm water and a flannel? Magdalene said the words in an affirmative tone, hoping it would bring Lisa out of her shock.

"Let's clean her, and if you could bring the holdall from the car, let's try and get some food into her," she called out. "You ok?"

Lisa nodded, obeying, and brought a bowl of warm water and a sponge to wipe the child's face. She went to the kitchen to warm some milk and heat up a jar of food in the microwave from the bag she had collected from the car.

Magdalene gently caressed the little girl's face. She was still gripping the stinking baby's bottle and she pulled it gently from her mouth, which made the child stir but she had no energy to protest. Lisa came in with the bottle of warm milk and Magdalene propped a cushion under it so that the child could drink from it without moving.

And so, here was where these two women let the child stay each day, comforting, caressing and feeding the little girl, building her strength until she was strong enough to be carried to the bath. Lisa cut her crusty hair short and they put bubbles in the water with rubber ducks and other toys to help to make it a fun experience, but they still had to support her weak and tiny body.

After a few weeks they introduced more jars of baby food to her bland milky diet and took it in turns to feed the gooey substance to the little girl, whose cheeks were becoming pink and whose eyes were becoming less cloudy. After four weeks the child could sit up supporting herself, and after two months she could sit in her special chair at the table.

It was at this time that Magdalene started her new job, which she loved, but in half her mind she was always thinking about coming home and hearing from Lisa about the improvements in their little girl. During her lunch break she would use her computer and go on the internet to look at stages of child development and she tried to work out exactly how old the child was, but it was impossible to say because she was so thin and small. As a computer analyst Magdalene was frustrated by not being able to work out things about the child in a logical way, so between them, Lisa and Magdalene decided that she was 18 months old or thereabouts. She was on the lowest percentile but this was understandable as she had been half starved. Magdalene had to look up on Google how to get rid of hair lice as the child was covered in them, but not just in her hair; there seemed to be things living on her skin too. They burned the blanket.

After three months the child's development took a turn and one day when Magdalene arrived home Lisa was smiling from ear to ear.

"Oh Mags, wait 'til you see this," she said as she turned and tickled the little girl under her chin, who responded with a chuckle, a real live chortle. Lisa laughed and Magdalene laughed, and the little girl chuckled as she was tickled some more. She chuckled more until all three were crying with joy and laughter in the warm kitchen in the snug happy cottage.

It was unlike the lovers to argue or even disagree but neither could decide what to name the little girl. Eventually, after some pouting and sulking it was decided that they would call her Maria. They also made a big decision. Magdalene would be the one who would say that she was Maria's mother. Magdalene had always liked *The Sound of Music* and that's why she chose the name Maria. Magdalene also chose Maria's surname, Amari.

'Maria Amari,' a word-play on her name.

Magdalene repeatedly said 'Maria, Maria' to her new charge and sang, 'How do you solve a problem like Maria?' Then one day she sang the words so loudly that Maria looked up at her.

"Good girl Maria," said Magdalene. "See, she knows her name now." She spoke to Lisa but she was looking at Maria. "Maria, Maria, Maria".

Lisa had given up calling the child anything else as she knew only too well Magdalene's determination, so she didn't bother to argue or protest and secretly thought that the name suited the child.

Maria grew and during that time no one thought about her real mother. It was as if that period of their lives had never existed.

Because they had decided that Magdalene was going to be the birth mother, they decided to tell people, if asked, that Lisa was the live-in nanny. This was perfectly acceptable, as Magdalene had a high-powered job in London and as Lisa's work was part-time, this concept would fit in around caring for Maria and perhaps avoid raising any suspicion.

Lisa hadn't built up any clients as her time was taken up with caring for Maria but as each day passed she dreaded the thought of taking her outside, never mind to some stranger's house for a piano tuning. Maria had never left the cottage since they had brought her there six months before. They were not ready, and although they both knew that they could not hide her away forever, each one of them was subconsciously putting the moment off.

The cottage was looking homely. Magdalene had treated Lisa to a new piano, an upright one as the rooms were too small for any other version. It sat in the front sitting room and in the early evenings, as winter drew near, the lovers played duets together. Maria would bang on her toys in some sort of harmony with a plastic hammer in her safe new world on her play blanket, chubby and pink beside the guarded log fire, all clean and rosy. One day, whilst the lovers played, she got up and took a few steps towards the piano and hit down hard on the keys with her plastic hammer. She laughed and wobbled and sat back down on her bottom, Magdalene and Lisa kissed and hugged each other and persuaded Maria to try and do it again. They cajoled her and watched in admiration at the first steps of their little girl since they had stolen her away, and since the first time Magdalene had watched Maria stagger determinedly to the door clinging to her wretched mother.

"I think she must be nearly two now, you know," said Lisa as she and Magdalene ate supper. Maria Amari was bathed and tucked up in bed. Lisa had read her a story about three little bears and had sung a lullaby to the twinkle of a bedtime musical clown that hung from her cot side.

"Can you pick up a cake from Marks and Spencer on the way home?" Lisa asked. "It's Saturday tomorrow, we could have a tea party and it's also the shortest day, 21st December. Let's make it Maria's birthday? What do you think?" she enquired.

Magdalene felt tired as she traipsed around Marks and Spencer's but soon cheered up when she found the range of cakes. She loved cake and there was a sponge cake with bright pink icing with ballerinas on the top. *How lovely*, she thought. *It's great having a child. Just think of the things that we can do now that we have childish excuses? Pantomimes, cinema trips, theme parks and picnics,* she thought. But then she thought it would mean taking Maria outside. Magdalene resolved to be strong and that as it was nearly Christmas, she and Lisa would take Maria out for the first time to see the tree on the village green. As it was a public area people might not feel obliged to ask too many questions. She had read about the community event in the village newsletter, there was going to be carol singing and mulled wine. Lisa would love it! And then she thought that Lisa would feel apprehensive too. She knew that Maria's main development was due to Lisa's dedication of care and that a strong bond was growing between them. Magdalene wasn't jealous or even envious, she just wished that she could have more time with Maria. Still, it was Christmas holidays soon and she was looking forward to Christmas Day and marvelled at how different this Christmas was going to be compared to this time last year when she had left the courtroom as a divorced woman, and the bleakness she had seen in her ex-husband's eyes. Snapping herself out of her morbid thoughts she quickly became cheery with the thought of going home to her partner and child.

"I love the cake, darling," Lisa said as she loaded the dish washer after supper. Did you buy some candles? We only need two."

Magdalene entered the kitchen, glass of wine in her hand.

"Oh bugger, candles, bloody hell! Aren't there any with the cake?"

Lisa checked and there wasn't. "I'll go to the village store in the morning and get some," she said. "Only two candles, not fork handles," which made Magdalene laugh. "The Two Ronnie's – ha, ha, fork handles, four candles," Magdalene said aloud as she kissed Lisa on the head. "I love you," she said.

"I love you too," said Lisa.

Chapter 4

The morning dawned with a low hanging mist across the valley, where the tips of green hills shuddered above as a chilly wind blew the remains of leaves across the waking landscape.

Lisa and Magdalene were excited, more so than Maria, who really had no idea about what was going to happen.

After lunch, when the misty light was at its best, between them the women wrapped Maria in a warm coat, boots, scarf, hat and mittens, both chatting excitingly about going outside.

Maria stood dutifully, watching the women with her large dark eyes now bright and clear. "Out thide," she said.

Magdalene and Lisa stopped and stared at each other. Lisa kissed Magdalene on the cheek and turned to Maria. "Outside," she said. "Maria, say outside," she repeated emphasising the 's'.

"Out thide," said Maria and pointed at the door.

"It's fate," said Magdalene. "She wants to go outside. Her first words to us, can you believe it?"

Villagers, wrapped against the chill, were making their way to the village green where the Christmas tree twinkled with merry fairy lights.

Lisa pushed the pushchair and Magdalene walked alongside, happily chatting to Maria explaining that she was going to see a Christmas tree.

"Tree," said Maria provoking each woman to shout, "Clever girl", and "tree".

"Ah, a child's first words are just heavenly, are they not, don't you think?" asked a woman with bobbed grey hair, slightly pink cheeks and a smile blessed with the warmth of her God. She was cheerily chatting to the two new women of the village who were so intently listening to the child speak that they had not noticed her drawing nearer along the cobbled street. Each stopped and looked surprised.

"Hello, I'm the Vicar, sorry not to have called to say Hi but terribly busy this time of year, as one would expect and really did not want to disturb before, thought to give you a chance to settle in don't you know?" Her voice was crisp and precise and clipped with well-educated English tones.

Magdalene smiled at the Vicar. She was used to dealing with religious types, having spent a life surrounded by catholic priests, but felt enlightened by this woman of the church, the Church of England.

"Oh, how kind of you to think of us," said Magdalene, her eyes bright and warm.

The vicar viewed the pair and quickly made her assumptions. Being a lesbian herself she figured that the two women were more than just a pair of friends but gave no indication of her thoughts. She was well-used to keeping those to herself. She was not 'out' and felt her life was better lived that way. She had decided a long time ago that she would be married to God. Sometimes she reprimanded herself for not coming out and being brave or even indeed having a partner in her younger years, but then she would consider where she was in her life and felt satisfied with her relationship with God. That was enough for her now.

"Oh God, where are our manners," said Magdalene. "I'm Magdalene, and this is my Nanny, Lisa and this chatty little girl is my daughter Maria. "How do you do?" The three women shook hands and the vicar, whom they discovered was called Wendy, continued to walk with them towards the huge tree and the gathering crowd.

"Singing is bloody awful, of course," Wendy said. We have one villager, Monica, who seems to think that she has been given a soprano voice likened to the great Dame Kiri te Kanawa. I think rather more she should be likened to fingernails running down a chalkboard but one does not want to disappoint or discourage the poor old girl. She was widowed recently and the Christmas Carol service and the Am. Dram. productions are all that keep her going, poor thing. She appears to have every malady disorder that God has ever created! Here's a tip, bring some earplugs next year! I'll visit soon, I love tea but no cake as I have far too much of that! Cheerio, and do try to enjoy the concert." Wendy dashed the triptych a wide smile and went to join her choir.

Maria sat excitedly in her posh pushchair which cost the same as a small second-hand car. She marvelled at the tree and its sparkle, at the humdrum of people, the cold pricking her ears, the snug of her favourite blanket, 'blanky' and listened soundly and with years advanced of her short life, she listened most wisely to the tune of the singing and the range of noises pouring forth from the mouths of the people circled together.

Running around were two young boys, chasing and bashing each other in the way that young boys do, with violence, but with acceptance and hurting but not really hurting. Their parents seemed oblivious, or rather more used to the scene playing out before them. After the singing had ended the father scooped the two boys up and carried them reluctantly under the crook of each arm. They continued to wrestle and joust, and as they came closer Maria noticed that they were identical to each other. Her little eyes shone and she screamed out, arousing the attention of Lisa. Magdalene was talking to the twins' mother who was telling her about the local playgroup and she was saying how lovely it was to have another child in the village. Would it be possible to make a play-date for her twins and Maria?

Magdalene was explaining that Lisa was her nanny and introduced her. Lisa stood up from her crouching position where she had been attending to Maria's outburst.

33

"Lisa is an excellent piano-tuner, so if you need her services she can bring Maria along to play with the boys too."

Walking back towards home, Lisa was cross. "What on earth were you saying to that dreadful woman about me piano-tuning and taking Maria around to their home to play with those awful unruly boys?"

"She's not dreadful, Lisa, she seemed really nice. She used to work in the city along with her husband but has just given up as the childcare was too expensive and she wants to spend more time with her boys. It will be great for Maria to have some friends. I heard her scream with delight when she spotted the twins. We can't deprive her of other children's company. We need to initiate ourselves into our community and I really think that if we do that, then people are less likely to have suspicions about us than if we continue to hide ourselves away, don't you agree?"

Lisa nodded but she wasn't sure.

"Oh come on Leese," Magdalene said. "They can be your first clients as they have a piano that wants tuning and they want the boys to have lessons too. You can take Maria and at least you can keep your eye on her whilst you are there. I think you should take her to the little nursery, too. It's only twice a week for a couple of hours in the village hall. Come on darling, don't be grumpy, you knew this time would come. You can do it, we can both do it."

Lisa nipped to the village shop and bought two bright candles for the cake and a bottle of champagne. "Sod it," she thought. "It's our child's first birthday celebration together and I need to snap out of this mood. Let's sod the expense and have some champagne to celebrate. Mags won't mind and I guess it will cheer me up." She had already got to know the interested and flirty shopkeeper whose wife seemed as hard as nails and seemed to resent every moment of her occupation. She had relayed her piano services to them and they had showed her where to put up her card to invite business from locals who needed pianos tuned and maybe some lessons. The shopkeeper, who was called Brian, informed Lisa that there were a lot of children in the village but most of the older ones went away to boarding schools or otherwise were at school for such a long day that they were unlikely to be seen around in term-time. Brian felt sure that she, Lisa, would easily pick up some business as there was, as far as he knew, no other piano teachers in the area. "Parents around here are most likely to want your services out of term-time", he had told her, "or, at weekends." Lisa was fine about those arrangements and left her card with her details on.

At home Mags had made some dainty sandwiches with the crusts cut off and put out some coloured iced biscuits, laid on the table. Lisa put the champagne in the fridge and placed two candles on the cake. The women sang happy birthday to Maria and she giggled and sang along, well not quite as she did not know the words, but the tune was no problem to her and she hummed and squealed. When the cake came she surmounted her joy by ramming as much cake as she could into her little mouth. Both women had to fish some out and entice her to eat little pieces. They lit and re-lit the two pink candles until they thought Maria would die from laughing along with them too as she blew, blew and blew and giggled and giggled. Then when Maria was bathed and tucked up for the night and Magdalene and Lisa were snuggled together on the sofa sipping champagne, the house glowed with a sense of happiness from all who lived there.

Maria grew. Her hair grew thick and curly. Her large brown eyes were deep and wide; like the colour of muddy pools, yet they were clear and bright.

Whilst Maria played on her multi-coloured play-mat, Lisa noticed the gleam in her eyes when she chatted to her imaginary friend. Lisa was becoming aware that this was a common occurrence and that Maria seemed to go from a child who struggled to speak a few words to a child who barely stopped talking in the space of a few short months. Maria's imaginary friend seemed to somehow support her newly found language and she conversed constantly with her invisible companion.

By Lisa and Magdalene's reckoning Maria was now about two and a half or thereabouts, yet her use of words and sentence structure never ceased to surprise the two women.

Lisa noticed the advancement in Maria's speech as she spent almost every moment of her wakening hours with her.

One long and fine summer's day, when the windows were open but the air in the cottage was still, Lisa lay on the play-mat with Maria and began to help her make a jigsaw puzzle of fifty pieces, making up a farmyard scene of pigs, cows, a tractor and a farmer carrying buckets of feed. Between them they made a perfectly completed jigsaw in a very short space of time. Maria showed great hand-to-eye coordination and superb logical decisions moving the shapes around until she was sure where they fitted. In truth, Lisa barely helped.

A short and unsettling blast of air suddenly filled the family room which made the hairs on the back of Lisa's neck stand up. The floral patterned curtains fluttered wildly, and Lisa stood up to close the window. By the time she got to it the air was still again. Uncontrollably, a shiver ran down Lisa's back. She sensed someone or something had entered the room and turned to look around but there was only Maria sitting on her play-mat looking up beyond her, transfixed as if she was listening to someone in the middle distance.

Maria responded, "Mo, Mo!" "Mo, Mo, piano," she said smiling. "Let's play?"

Lisa gawped as Maria stood up and toddled to the upright piano where the top was now covered in magazines and discarded cosmetics and newspapers.

"Who's Mo, Mo?" asked Lisa.

Maria did not reply, she was focusing on toddling over to the piano and struggled to climb upon the piano stool. With her long fingers she picked out keys and with both hands moving she played, 'Twinkle, Twinkle Little Star'. She was chuckling and her brown curls bobbed up and down as she nimbly played the key notes again.

Rooted to the spot, Lisa exclaimed, "Maria, Maria!" Her words were loud and directive. She could not help but shout the words at Maria. She felt strange and she thought the situation was very peculiar.

Maria turned, her face crumpled and she began to cry. Lisa rushed to sit beside her in the small space left on the piano stool.

"Oh Maria, sorry, sorry," she said as she cuddled her. "I didn't mean to scare you, there, there, it's OK." She began to distract Maria from her tears by asking her to play it again, telling Maria what a clever and good girl she was.

With this encouragement Maria repeated the tune and Lisa clapped her hands and gave words of praise, "Clever girl!"

Picking out the keys in a lower scale Maria and Lisa played the whole tune through together. Maria was beaming. At the end Lisa put her arm around Maria and asked,

"Who taught you that, Maria?"

"Mo, Mo" said Maria.

"Is Mo, Mo your friend?" asked Lisa.

Maria nodded her head.

"Yes, Mo, Mo plays the piano and I am going to play the piano too!"

"Just like me?" said Lisa.

"No" said Maria. "Just like Mo, Mo."

Lisa placed Maria on the play-mat and turned on the television, finding the children's channel. Luckily Maria's favourite programme about a pig family was showing and this occupied her whilst Lisa made herself a strong cup of coffee.

She wasn't sure how she was going to explain to Magdalene that the child that they had abducted seemed to be a child genius, a prodigy influenced by her imaginary friend. However, Lisa thought that if Maria had got a talent then she had had lots of opportunities to hear Lisa play. She did often play nursery rhymes for Maria to sing along to so perhaps this is where she had learned the tune? She wasn't going to talk to

Mags about the odd feeling she had when Maria took it upon herself to play the piano that afternoon. Lisa put it down to the heat of the day.

When Magdalene arrived home with yet another purchase from a trip to a toy shop, bringing home a cuddly pink teddy, Lisa sat her down to speak with her after she had put Maria to bed.

"Mags, don't buy Maria any more toys, she has more than plenty and actually we are running out of space to keep them. You are spoiling her and the thing she plays the most with is her 'blanky'. And…oh, and the piano."

Lisa was unusually firm. They were sat together, Magdalene stretched out with her feet resting over Lisa's knees. There was a vintage comedy programme on the television that neither was really watching but now and again Magdalene let out a little snigger. She raised her head slightly at Lisa's tone.

"Lisa, what's wrong?" she asked.

Lisa explained to Magdalene that Maria was learning to play the piano under her tutelage and was showing exceptional talent for her young age.

"She plays with her imaginary friend called Mo, Mo," said Lisa.

Of course, Magdalene already knew about Maria's imaginary friend. She had included 'Mo, Mo' in their play times, serving fantasy meals to someone who wasn't there in the space on the play-mat between them.

Maria would screech with glee in their childish games and she would babble and gurgle to the vision of her own seeing.

Magdalene pulled her feet up from Lisa's knees. "Oh crikes," she said alarmingly, "Is this going to be a problem for us?" she asked.

"I don't know," said Lisa. "Lots of children have imaginary friends, I'm sure it's perfectly normal. But Mags, her piano playing is melodic and beautiful and natural. She has a gift. Since playing nursery rhymes she has progressed to 'Für

Elise' and to our reckoning she's not even three years old yet! She is reading the music too and she just hums and hums.

Tomorrow's Saturday, Mags, no swimming lesson, let's just sit down and listen together to her playing, I promise you will be astounded."

Magdalene reached over to hug Lisa and kissed her passionately. She felt Lisa's muscles relaxing in her arms.

Magdalene whispered to Lisa that they were a good team. She said that Lisa was doing a fantastic job and that Maria seemed to be the happiest little girl in the world. Hadn't they branched out into the community? What with the nursery sessions, the planned play-dates and the swimming lessons? Magdalene told Lisa that it was unlikely that at this point in time Maria's talent would be problematic. Everyone knew that Lisa could play the piano and so the fact that Maria was so good was self-explanatory, wasn't it?

Despite her soothing words Lisa could not help the butterflies in her stomach. Each of them had been pivotal in the abduction of a child. Lisa had often scanned the newspapers and local radio news stations to hear whether anything had ever been reported about the snatching of Maria. Nothing had ever reared its ugly head to discover them. She could not believe that they had both got away with it. A year had gone by and she admitted to herself that it would be hard to recognise Maria for the same desperate child that she was. Her development had been exponential. Each time she looked at their gorgeous little girl she knew the risk was worth it. If they had not taken her she may well be dead by now.

"She is a natural," said Lisa. "She is far more talented than me. She has been rehearsing a surprise for you."

Lisa kissed Magdalene before she could reply and moved her hands to stroke her breasts and softly kiss her neck. Using her tongue Lisa traced Magdalene's contours down to the delights between her moist thighs and she slowly brought Magdalene to an orgasm.

Magdalene murmured 'Für Elise, hey," and Lisa squeezed her tightly, and the two women continued to pleasure each other and made passionate love.

Chapter 5

The next day Maria played Für Elise and Magdalene was aghast at her talent. The sound that this small child was making was astounding to her and she could barely believe what she was hearing. Lisa gave her a knowing look as if to say, 'I told you so.'

Lisa watched closely how Maria developed. She was not short of toys, as Magdalene often bought her new ones, bringing home dolls, games and puzzles after work. Magdalene enjoyed shopping for them. She loved the big toy stores in London. It seemed to give her a purpose and she felt that the shopping was therapeutic and much more fun than scanning for clothes to fit her shapely body. She felt concerned about Lisa telling her to stop her impulsive purchasing and she guessed she was right. Maria certainly did seem to be more interested in playing the piano and she marvelled at the child they had stolen. She often thought what a coincidence it was that Lisa was so musical and that Maria seemed to be falling into her footsteps, but even brighter. She reasoned in her mind that she and Lisa should do something about Maria's prodigious ability but she didn't know what.

Lisa got into the habit of keeping Maria up so the two women could share the bath and bed routine together and took it in turns to read a bedtime story and tuck her in for the night.

Maria continued to grow. Her hair grew long. Her large brown eyes were deep and wide and hauntingly like her own mother's though this was never mentioned. The deep muddy-coloured pools shone brightly, gleaming with multi-coloured pigment of greens and violets especially when she chatted to her imaginary friend. At these moments Maria would reach out as if stroking someone's face and would talk fervently to someone who wasn't there. In a few short months Maria and her new-found friend conversed in mutual conspiracy.

Lisa took Maria to the twin's house with some apprehension. She felt nervous and afraid that she may give away some part of their secret. She valued her life and her happiness so much that the night before she barely slept. Magdalene had done her best to comfort her, but as she always had to get up so early for her morning commute to London, Lisa did her best not to keep her awake with her worries.

Magdalene had told her that everything was going to be all right, that Maria needed to engage with other children and they couldn't always depend on each other all of the time. They both needed to make new friends as well as Maria and the twins' mother seemed so nice. "It will do you good, Lisa", Magdalene had told her. She had work colleagues and London for company but Lisa needed to get out. OK – what they had done would probably put them both in prison if anyone ever found out but as she had said before, that was more likely to happen if Lisa and Maria insisted on being locked away in their dear cottage which could become a prison in itself. Neither of them wanted that, they both agreed and although Lisa came around to Magdalene's ideas, she had a nagging doubt that would not leave her. Lisa thought that this was small comfort and lay awake watching the clock until Magdalene woke and got ready for work.

Lisa arrived at the stylish and symmetrical Georgian house. Coming from an orphanage she was in some awe as she entered the beautifully decorated home with its high ceilings and plastered mouldings. She was amazed that there seemed to be no existence of those unruly boys until she was led into the kitchen and family area. The mother of the two boys was called Helen, and as she filled the kettle and prepared tea served with carrot cake, Lisa let the room sink in; its atmosphere was light and airy.

There was a large cork board filled with drawings, paintings and play-date cards. The pictures were obviously completed by the terrible twins, whom she discovered were called Freddie and Peter.

The big island in the middle of the smartly attired kitchen area was brightly topped in polished granite and a large window with a striped patterned blind cut out the distant sunlight, where a vase of yellow daffodils gave some cheery colour. Beyond this area was a play area cum sitting area with a dining table placed with four chairs. Two folding windows opened out to a wide paved patio where raffia tables and seats peeked through green covers. There was the biggest television that Lisa had ever seen on the central wall, and a children's programme was showing with the volume blasting out so loudly that it was difficult to hear Helen's polite conversation as she enquired whether Lisa would care for sugar?

The two boys were sat together on a corner settee, wonderfully placid, watching the characters on the television. Lisa was bemused by this and sat next to them, placing Maria on her lap. Maria somehow seemed to slip into the ambience of the room and the boy's mood and she sat motionless, mimicking their concentration, not stirring or even making a sound.

However, as soon as the programme ended the atmosphere quickly changed to one of chaos. The boys leapt up seemingly to have only just realised that Maria was among them and began to bring out a range of toys to entice her off Lisa's knee to play together on the large rug.

Maria seemed happy to join in and squealed and chatted and in no time at all she had confirmed the hierarchy within the group, and she was most definitely at the top. The boys attentively did everything that she ordered them to and this included dressing up in every article of clothing from the dressing up box and then upon her orders they were to follow her to march around the kitchen table again and again and again. Each boy following, slipping over trailing clothes and picking themselves up to keep up with Maria until she stopped and said that she was bored with that game and she wanted to go out into the garden to play, as she looked at Lisa for approval.

Lisa looked anxiously at Helen who soon reassured her that the garden was completely safe and that they could keep an eye on the children from where they were sitting.

Catching the boys before they entered the garden, Lisa helped Helen undress them down to their normal clothes whilst Maria was already ahead of them claiming a swing seat to herself with her legs out, humming a Mozart piano concerto as she swung back and forth. The boys joined her, jostling for the seat next to her.

"Girls are so much more advanced, don't you think?" said Helen.

Lisa lifted her gaze from the children to Helen, who was now sitting on the edge of the sofa turned to face Lisa.

"Oh, yes," she said. "Oh yes," she said a little louder, enforcing her attention to Helen smiling.

Helen was sipping her tea but didn't touch her cake. She was very thin and Lisa guessed that she probably hardly had any time to eat and that it was no wonder, really, with those twins.

"God, I'm exhausted," said Helen. "Those two never seem to sleep through the night. If one wakes up then the other wakes up too. Tony keeps asking for another baby! Can you believe it? I've told him no chance, of course. He just loves those boys and relishes the weekends where he can teach them cricket and football in the garden and half drowns them in the swimming pool. I think I've seen you there in the class before us?" she added. "Which means that they are so boisterous and wound up by Monday it takes me a week to calm them down again, only for him to go through the whole process the next weekend. Oh, I give up!"

Lisa nodded as Helen spoke. She had some sympathies for Helen as she had seen the way her husband had played with the boys on the village green at Christmas. Helen spoke rather quickly, and Lisa thought that this was probably because she needed to say as much as she could before one of the boys grabbed her attention again. Anyway, for now the children were playing really well and Lisa chewed on the delicious cake. She noticed the cake box on the side was from Fortnum and Mason.

"Well," said Helen. "They seem to be playing awfully well don't they? How lovely that you have moved here. So sorry I've not been able to catch up at the nursery in the village hall, but dropping the boys off twice a week means that at least I can get some shopping in and I even sometimes manage to get my hair done. It's simply heaven, and time not to waste. I'm sure you know what I mean? No? You probably don't as I have double the trouble of course. Anyway, only a year or so and the boys will be off to school. I'm looking forward to that. If you do the crime you have to do the time, hey?"

Lisa tittered but Helen didn't seem to be laughing. She looked far away. Rousing herself, Helen said,

"Would you like to see the piano? It's rather grand in every sense of the word. It used to belong to Tony's great, great, oh I don't know how many great grandfathers, who, according to family legend, was taught how to play it by Mozart. I don't think that can be true, do you? I am sure it would be very different from the one we have here, and what in the world would Mozart be doing in England?"

Lisa realised that Helen was directing the questions to herself but she answered them anyway.

"Some pianos are very old and over the years have been changed and adapted, but there really won't be much left of the original instrument that your husband's great, hmm, great and so on grandfather had, but Mozart did come to England, you know. I recall reading somewhere that he came here as a child prodigy..." (The word prodigy made her think of Maria and she shuddered, but wasn't sure why) "…with his mother and father and sister."

"Mozart had a sister?" enquired Helen.

"Yes, he did," Lisa said. "Nannerl, she was a very talented and gifted musician who suffered great musical oppression for being a woman in her time. It's mostly down to her that Mozart's music survives. Some reports say that she was as talented as Mozart and that she composed too, but her father was set against her becoming anything of a performer. Mozart was the young boy whom he wished to showcase to the aristocracy of Europe. It was much more lucrative to have a younger boy child perform."

"How sad," Helen said. "Not surprising."

"Boys!" she bellowed into the garden. "I'm just taking Lisa to the sitting room to tune the piano. All OK?"

Helen did not wait for an answer but got up to show Lisa the way to the piano, back up the stairs to the splendid sitting room.

Old family portraits hung around the room, some dark and in need of a clean, yet the room was light and spacious with a high ceiling and sparkly central chandelier and matching smaller wall lights. The walls and carpet were dangerously pale, a sort of tepid milk colour, and the curtains were green and patterned in a William Morris print. Helen had picked out the same green for the accessories, the plump cushions on the two majestic sofas and the vases that sat on two elaborate side tables which held large lilies; their perfume filled the room.

Lisa had always associated lilies with funerals but she felt that the flowers suited the room and helped to give the design of the room the proportion that the Georgian splendour deserved. It was very clear to Lisa that the 'boys' were not allowed in here as the room was tidy and almost had the look of a show home, as it looked unlived in.

Seeing the piano, she guessed, although admitting to herself that she was no expert, that the piano was not as old as her husband's family obviously thought it was. It was an antique and had an excellent maker's name engraved in gold on the inside of the lid, which was open. This dismayed Lisa somewhat as this would only encourage dust to settle in between the keys. *Helen should take better care of it,* she thought, and then chastised herself for thinking it as this tired woman in front of her probably did not have the time to worry about such things owing to her 'boys'.

"What a lovely room," said Lisa. "And the piano is beautiful. I've spied the maker's name – you are so lucky to have this. May I play it?"

"Be my guest," said Helen. "I'm going to make some lunch, would you like to stay? Likely to be something simple, but do join us. I'll give you a shout when it's ready. Don't worry about Maria, I'll keep my eye on the children."

Lisa could not answer as Helen's voice was drifting along the hall as she made her way to the family room to prepare lunch for them all.

Lisa sat at the piano and stroked it. She kissed the middle 'c' and its cold ivory key kissed her back in a sensuous tone as she gently pressed it down with her long right hand thumb. The piano vibrated smoothly and she heard the ebony creak into submission as she played the short burst of Grieg's Arietta op. 12/1. She followed this with another Grieg, his waltz op. 12/2. Lisa loved Grieg. It was these two pieces that she had first learned to play off by heart.

Her inner ear listened unconsciously to hear if Helen needed her yet, but as there was only the sound of a knife on a chopping board, she chose to play another Grieg. This time she let herself be drawn into the arms of this beautiful masterpiece of a piano and her hips swayed ever so slightly as she began to touch the keys and play part of his 'To Spring' op. 43/6. She knew every key, every tome, and every soulful movement of her hands to create the Erotic op. 43/5 and by now she could only hear Grieg's voice, melodious in her mind.

Helen stood at the door, watching Lisa, sensing not to speak until Lisa had finished playing. Even then she waited a moment for Lisa to place her hands on her lap.

"That was incredible, Lisa. I have never heard that piano being played so beautifully before. You'd better not let the vicar hear you playing as she will summon you up for one of her concerts before you can say 'no'. What was that you were playing?"

"Some Grieg," said Lisa. "Do you need a hand in the kitchen?"

"Oh, no, it's fine, come on down, lunch is ready and we can call the children in to wash their hands..."

Over a small but healthy lunch Lisa had more opportunity to engage in conversation with Helen. Helen seemed more relaxed in her company and together the women chit-chatted about motherhood's ups and downs and scooped food off the table to supply the infants with nourishment.

In this shared familiarity Helen and Lisa became friends.

Chapter 6

Lisa returned Helen's kindness by inviting her and the twins over for lunch the following week, and this arrangement continued from time to time. Frequently, Lisa would avoid answering Helen's questions about Magdalene, particularly about childbirth, by distracting Helen into conversations about her own childbirth which she was very proud of, having giving birth to the twins naturally. Lisa reminded herself that she and Mags would have to, at some point, agree by which method of childbirth Maria had been born. Perhaps it would be best to say that Magdalene had given birth to Maria naturally as she had no caesarean scar, not that anyone but she would ever see it. However, she thought thinking of every eventuality, if Mags ever needed to see the village doctor he would notice if she didn't have a scar.

Thoughts were tumbling through Lisa's head and she decided that it would be a good idea to write everything down so that the two women would never forget their version of childbirth events. Thinking ahead, it would be best for them to have the same story should Maria ever ask them someday. They would have to agree her birth weight, and as she was quite small she would have to research on the internet what Maria's birth weight could have been. *Five or six pounds,* she thought. Was this light weight possible for someone like Mags to give birth to? Mags was such a healthy woman, a little on the chubby side, but she had the energy of a woman half her age. The more Lisa thought about things the more her head spun until she could not stand it anymore. She spoke to Magdalene about it one evening when the summer's sun was lingering in the open window and the heat of the day could still be smelled in the drifts coming through from the garden. Lisa had planted night-scented stocks under the kitchen window along with mint and herbs, and their fragrance seeped through the old cottage walls.

As ever, Magdalene was organised and efficient in her actions and came up with a feasible story:

"Let's say," said Magdalene, "that I had not realised I was pregnant when I split up from Kevin. I may even say that Maria isn't his she just came along due to some one night stand, if anyone needs any detail.

I'd guess Maria weighed 6lbs and 8oz which is not a bad weight at all under the circumstances."

She elaborated that she had a natural birth and a couple of stitches and the labour lasted for 12 hours.

As Magdalene spoke, Lisa wrote this all down and together they rehearsed and rehearsed the words, asking questions of each other to make sure that they had got the story right.

They agreed that if anyone asked, Magdalene would say that she found herself on her own with the baby and advertised for a nanny and along came Lisa.

"That sounds quite plausible you know, Leese. Anyway, I don't think people will ask too much, it's none of their business. If people are that nosy then you'll just have to say that you don't know, as I'm her mother, after all."

"Maria may ask us one day, you know. It's good to be sure about stuff," Lisa said pointedly. There was a quiet determination in her voice and Magdalene picked up a tremble. *Perhaps she is thinking too deeply about this*, Magdalene thought, and wished that Lisa would stop worrying. Her anxiety didn't show but Magdalene knew her well enough to detect a fear within her.

Magdalene kept her gaze on Lisa. Her slim body and her ivory coloured skin reminded her of the keys on the piano. She always looked gorgeous, even on a bad day when she would whisk her hair into a knot on the top of her head. She wore a pale pink lipstick with no other make-up, which she didn't need. Her lower arms were covered in blonde hairs and her smile was like honey. Magdalene lusted for her and watched Lisa's stooped head over her notebook penning the words of their making in sequence of time.

"Lisa, are you ok with this? Look, I know that is what women love to discuss at great length but you can easily avoid stuff like this if you just say that I am her mother and that you don't really know. You are Maria's nanny after all."

Lisa was not sure whether Magdalene was inferring that she was inferior to Mags who was the chosen birth mother, but did not wish to quarrel so continued to write in her notebook. Lisa knew in that moment that the unspoken truth between them was looming but she chose to ignore the chance that Magdalene was giving her for them to speak of it.

"Fine, it's all here in this book and so it will remain. Fine Magdalene, it's fine."

Then she raised her head and said,

"Of course, Mags, you are right. It's no one else's business but our own. I am just so worried that I may trip up one day."

Magdalene softened her voice. "You'll never trip up, Lisa, because you know how much this means to all of us. Shall I make some tea? No, wine, I'll open some wine."

After the weekend Lisa was unfaltering in her decision to concentrate on Maria's musical gifts. She had contemplated whether she was now the right person to be teaching Maria as she advanced in her technique and sight-reading. She was not sure who else she could ask. As far as she was aware there was no one else in the area. In a few months Maria would be celebrating her third birthday. She was truly amazing and natural in her piano playing for her age. Lisa felt that she needed to be stretched and challenged.

That morning Lisa found her violin, packed and stored away in the cupboard under the stairs. She had been nowhere near it for many years and it was badly out of tune. Going into the front sitting room, Lisa encouraged Maria to sit on the rug in front of the fireplace where she was contently playing hide and seek with her 'blanky', which she was covering over her imaginary playmate and squealing as her invisible friend cried 'Boo'!

Lisa had gleaned that Maria's friend was a man. He was called Mo, Mo and showed Maria how to play the piano. Maria said that she always knew when he was in the room because he smelled of marzipan. Lisa was never quite sure whether she too could smell almonds in the room during those times. Sometimes she pinched herself for being so accepting of the situation. But as Maria believed in her imaginary friend to an extraordinary degree, Lisa resolved that she would too just to please Maria. At times she found herself engaging Mo, Mo in her music teaching. She had the advantage over Maria as she would say, 'But Mo, Mo wants you to do it like this' and Maria would comply.

Lisa tuned the violin and began to play a version of Bach's 'Arioso' from Cantata No. 156, but not very well as she could not recall it all.

Maria abruptly stopped playing with Mo, Mo and asked Lisa who had composed the piece she was playing.

"This is a piece by Bach," Lisa explained. "I don't remember it very well but I am sure that I have the music somewhere. Would you like to learn to play the violin, Maria?"

"Yes," said Maria. She had been staring up at Lisa as she played the violin before her in a rustic fashion. Maria knew that the tune was not quite perfect but she was enjoying the sound.

"But I only want to play Mo, Mo's music. He says that I can play the violin and he will teach me, and that you are not to concern yourself with my playing, Lisa. He is my Maestro, not you. You are adequate but Mo, Mo says I need to learn with him as he is the Maestro. Leave the violin with me, please, and go to the kitchen room and read for a little while. I'll call you in when I'm ready."

Lisa was affronted by Maria's coolness towards her and was shaken by her dismissal. Lately, she wondered where Maria had learned words that she had not discussed with her. Lisa felt that there was a shadow in the room. She was about to reply but Maria was pushing her bottom out of the room with adult strength.

Finding that she was standing on the other side of the door, Lisa's emotions turned to fury. She returned to the sitting room and picked up Maria forcefully, holding her down and dragging her into her arms.

"You precocious and spoiled little girl," Lisa roared the words.

Maria began to scream and shout and wriggled and scratched out at Lisa but Lisa's fortitude was not weakening and she took Maria to her room, almost threw on her bed and told her to stay there until she was told she could come out. Slamming the door behind her she heard Maria's anger rising as she flung toys and books around the room. Ten minutes later the room went quiet and when Lisa checked on her she was fast asleep, her temper spent.

Lisa was shocked at her own reaction to Maria's outburst and when she went back to the family room she shouted, 'Fuck Off, Mo, Mo!'

She had calmed her emotions by sitting quietly and rewinding what had just happened in her mind, replaying it all like a film in slow motion. She did not notice the time passing. She put on a CD of Mozart's piano concerto No.23 in A, K488 Adagio, and softly cried. This piece comforted her and she dozed off. After about two hours Lisa went to wake Maria.

It was unlike her to sleep for so long and when she woke Maria was burning up with a fever, and Lisa carried her downstairs. She took her temperature which was high and checked her back and torso where she found spots. Lots of red, white-tipped spots. Laying Maria on one of the sofas and gently covering her with a tartan throw, she rang Helen.

"Hi Helen, Lisa here. Yes, yes fine I'm fine thanks. And you?" Lisa wasn't really listening to Helen but was waiting for an opportunity to ask Helen about Maria's spots.

"The boys have got chicken pox, sorry I should have said but their spots only came out a few days ago, I had no idea as they were both as loud and boisterous as usual. I think some of the other children from the nursery have had it too. Just children's medicine and calamine I'm afraid, for a week or two. My mother-in-law is coming over tomorrow so let me know if you need anything from the shop and I can pick it up for you, I'll need a break to get away from her so I could drop in, OK?"

"Phew, that's a relief, chicken pox, I see. Yes, great, see you tomorrow sometime. Ooh, could you fetch some calamine and cotton wool please? Cheers. Bye."

Lisa ran the cold tap and soaked a sponge, which she dabbed on Maria's hot and blotchy skin. She kissed her forehead.

"Sorry my love, for shouting at you."

Maria snuggled beneath her 'blanky' and dozed off.

Lisa did not mention the incident to Magdalene as part of her thought that it was best forgotten. She felt rather ridiculous for being jealous of an imaginary friend but deep inside she felt uncomfortable and hoped that Maria's over-active imagination and outburst was because of her high temperature and nothing else. For now, she did not want to think about the nothing else.

Chapter 7

Lisa was lazily reclining on one of the large couches whilst Magdalene prepared lunch. The kitchen was on view from the comfy family area where the furnishings hugged the smoothness of the room. Maria had recovered from her bout of chicken pox and was at a play-date with the twins. This was a change for a Saturday, but Helen had suggested it as the children had been apart for so long.

Lisa was jolted swiftly from her thoughts as Magdalene asked her whether she wanted tea or coffee.

Lisa and Magdalene sat together at their little table, the vacant space where Maria normally sat yawning out at them like a huge crevice.

"It's really weird, our little girl not being here, don't you think, Lisa? I mean, don't get me wrong, it's lovely for us to have this time together but I am really missing her."

"It's only been an hour," Lisa replied. "Magdalene..." She made her voice quieter. "Magdalene, Maria has prodigious talent and well, I think I have worked out who her imaginary friend is."

"Who Maria thinks her imaginary friend is? Don't be so ridiculous Lisa. It's no one in particular, it's all in her mind. Really, don't try to make a big deal out of this, Lisa."

"But Magdalene!" Lisa cried. "I am serious. Honestly, I think that I have worked it all out. Maria's friend is Mozart. He comes to her. Look, listen..." Lisa made her voice quieter sensing that Magdalene was becoming angry. "I've done some research and it seems that Mozart took a lot of laudanum for his illness and laudanum smells like almonds or marzipan. When he is in the room, there is a lingering odour that pervades our house, there is a drabness to it, I smell it too, Magdalene."

Lisa was not expecting Magdalene's response. She stood up and loomed over Lisa, seeming taller than usual. Her face was a pinkish/purple and she was seething.

For Magdalene the whole thing was illogical and she could not get over Lisa being dragged into Maria's fantasy world. Magdalene rationalised events, there was no rhyme or reason for Lisa to think that their house was being visited by a dead composer. It was stupid.

She bellowed at Lisa. "Nonsense! Nonsense, Lisa! Don't be so ridiculous! She's a little girl for God's sake! She's entitled to her imagination Lisa, but not you. Don't be so silly and daft. Marzipan, Jesus, who ever heard anything so foolish!"

Lisa was beginning to cry and to be fearful of Magdalene. She had never seen her so angry. Maria's musicality was like an elephant in the room. As soon as she had broached the subject of her imaginary friend, Magdalene's reactions were bizarre and unexpected to her.

Magdalene snatched her car keys from the kitchen counter and stormed off to her car, slamming the door behind her. Lisa heard her drive off and change gear as she sped off down the country lane as the sound faded.

Later that day when Maria was home and picking out the Bach piece on the violin in the front sitting room, Magdalene returned home with flowers, champagne and chocolates and some brightly coloured sweets for Maria.

"Playing the Bach, then?" Magdalene enquired.

"Yes," said Maria. "Magdalene said that if I learn the Bach then she will buy me some Mozart Violin sheets. She said that we can learn the Violin Sonata in E minor together."

"Well, that's ambitious but I expect you'll master it in no time. Here are some sweeties for being a good girl and listening to Lisa about the Bach."

"Thank you, mummy."

Magdalene had twitched slightly at the mention of Mozart's name but said nothing. Returning to the family room she found Lisa filling the kettle. She put her arms around her and kissed her neck.

"I'm so bloody sorry," she said. She turned Lisa around to face her and kissed her tenderly on the mouth, on her neck, on her forehead. The couple exchanged loving words and caressed and stroked each other until Lisa pulled away.

"We have to talk about this, Magdalene."

"I know."

"Tomorrow then?"

"Yes, tomorrow."

As they chatted the diffused sunlight was falling through the long window. Lisa wanted to discuss their daughter's musical talents and what, as a couple, they should do about her friend, imaginary or not. She had figured out that Magdalene was struggling to come to terms with the consequences and underpinning it all was her fear of losing Maria. Her analytical brain was not cross wired to any creativity. Things were always black and white in her mind. This was going to be difficult.

In the evening when Maria was tucked up in bed, Magdalene opened the champagne. It tasted bitter to Lisa. As she sipped it her mind was racing. That night, for the first time, when Magdalene crept in bed beside her, she pretended to be asleep. Lisa was in deep thought, the links in the chain gave Lisa a troubled sensation, holding them there in her head, trying to make certain of the evidence behind her own eyes as she reasoned with herself about Maria.

It was Sunday and the church bells rang out through a crisp autumn morning. The household had eaten breakfast and were leisurely engaged in reading papers, drinking filter coffee and playing childish pursuits. Maria and Magdalene were playing snakes and ladders at the table where a jug was filled with late meadow flowers. The delicate room was reminiscent of many chocolate box cottages in the county and today the air felt drowsy.

Gradually the drowsiness lifted and Magdalene and Maria called Lisa to sit with them. Maria, having won the snakes and ladders, was keen to see what entertainment was lined up for her next.

"Maria," Magdalene said. Her eyes pierced through Maria.

"Who is your friend?" She didn't state 'imaginary' as she had come to realise that her friend was very real to her.

"What's his name, darling?"

"Mo, Mo."

Her attractive face gave no expression.

"That's what you call him, darling, but what is his real name? What shall mummy and Lisa call him? We'd like to know so that we can be his friends too." She spoke in a meditatively way to entice the revelation out of Maria.

Maria contested this point saying that he was *her* friend and only hers. After some coaxing she came around.

"If you must know, his name is Mozart. Johannes Chrysostomus Wolfgangus Theophilus Mozart."

Chapter 8

In the last blue days of autumn and when Christmas items were beginning to appear on shop shelves, Lisa spent at least four hours in each day teaching Maria the Grieg piece on the violin. She had progressed and as promised had been bought the Mozart Violin Sonata music. Lisa guessed that Maria would be keener to learn the Mozart.

When Maria was three Lisa and Magdalene held a small birthday party for her at the village hall and invited children from the day nursery to come along. Magdalene had hired a magician for entertainment and by the end of what seemed a dragged-out two hours all returned home exhausted. The following year had gone by plainly except that Maria's musical gifts grew stronger and the moments that she shared with Mozart became more regular.

As Lisa spent the most time with her, she had become accustomed to her competition in the tutelage field and accepted that Maria, for whatever reason and by what means she did not understand, was enjoying more time with her friend. Lisa knew when he was around because his scent pervaded the air and she would leave Maria to practise alone with him. The time in their cottage had flown by and Maria was now approaching her fourth birthday.

The Christmas tree on the village green had already gone up and villagers were rehearsing for the annual event around it.

The season had arrived imperceptibly and both Magdalene and Lisa had endless discussions about when Maria should attend school.

Lisa had reservations as she was sure that the school would ask for a birth certificate. Magdalene said that they would get around it by saying they had lost it with other belongings in the move to Kent. She felt sure that after a while the matter would be forgotten. Lisa wasn't so sure.

It was one of those days when the hours seem long and the sky is permanently grey that Maria was practising her violin sonata alone in the sitting room. Lisa was busying herself in the kitchen. She looked out of the window at the garden covered in brown rotting stems left over from another season and decided to go out and do some clipping and cutting. It was about 11 o'clock and the sky was tranquil. The house was breathless. Only the light feathery sound of Maria's violin lingered. She went out to tidy the little border under the kitchen window. Grabbing her secateurs from the garden shed, she began to trim and prune the tawny-rooted leftovers.

Meanwhile, the front door rapped. It was Wendy, the vicar who had decided to call on the two women that she had met beneath the Christmas tree a year or so ago. Of course, she had seen them at other occasions, the nursery Christmas play, the Harvest Festival and the village country show but somehow she felt she would like to get to know them better as they never came to church, and since she was passing...

No answer. She knocked again. Wendy heard music coming from the front room and peered through the window, expecting Lisa to be listening to a CD. She was surprised to see Maria plucking at a violin, her bow moving up and down next to her small body. Her gorgeous dark curls were tied up in a ponytail and her body swished in time to the harmony. She listened. Exquisite. *That child's a marvel, and a gift from God!* she exclaimed to herself.

Maria came out to find Lisa and told her someone was knocking at the door. *Why can't people use the bell?* Lisa thought as she got up to head back in the house. When she opened the door she saw the back of Wendy walking through the latch gate. She meant to call out but the words didn't come. Maria stood behind her and then turned back to her violin playing so that the music engulfed her, as if the visit was of no consequence. Little did either of them know the impending force of that moment.

The next day, Wendy called again. Tiny snowflakes had begun to fall, lacing the trees and ground with a promise that more would come soon. This time she noticed the bell and rang it ferociously. She could hear Maria playing and she intended to hear more. Lisa opened the door. Wendy noticed that she had spots of icing sugar on her apron and across her cheeks where she had wiped her hands.

"Hello" Wendy said.

"Hello Wendy. Do come in. I'm just making Maria's birthday cake. Excuse the mess. Maria, come through and you can have a drink too. Tea, Wendy?"

Once they were sat at the table and Lisa had made and poured tea out of charming flowery teacups, Wendy paused for thought.

"I'm so sorry not to have called earlier. Rather a large flock to tend to, I'm afraid."

Wendy's reference to her flock made Lisa squirm a little.

Wendy went on.

"I could not help hearing Maria playing the Mozart yesterday. I called, you know, but there was no answer."

Lisa felt like saying that she knew because she had seen her leaving but thought it best not to mention this, as she did not wish to seem rude.

"She has exceptional talent. Just glorious. How old is she now, four, five?" Wendy did not wait for Lisa to answer but continued,

"I have a suggestion, my dear. How lovely it would be if Maria could play at the Church Christmas Music Festival. It would be delightful and a refreshing change from Monica's screeches."

Wendy was silently praying to her God for her transgressions as she had deeper plans for Maria than she was prepared to tell to Lisa. She had been slightly suspicious of the two women and their relationship, not that this mattered at all, but she was perceptive enough to know that neither woman would welcome her interference. There was some gravity to her intentions and her intuition was telling her to keep them to herself.

Maria overheard Wendy and exclaimed that she would love to play in the church.

"There you are, my dear. It's providence that Maria should wish so wholeheartedly to come along and play for us."

Lisa looked Wendy in the eye. A judder passed over her before she spoke.

"Maria darling, we will have to check with mummy first."

"But I want to, I want to. Freddie and Peter will be there won't they, Wendy?"

Wendy shifted in her chair at being called Wendy by a little person.

"Don't get too excited Maria, we must ask mummy first."

Lisa continued her hard stare at Wendy, not looking at Maria as she spoke.

"Can we let you know? When is it exactly?"

"Oh, a couple of Sundays away. Five o'clock and the Women's Institute serve tea afterwards. It is really a rather lovely occasion and you don't have to be religious to come along, all are welcome."

Wendy drank her tea as Lisa sat in silence.

"Must be orff. Old Mr Perkins had a fall and can't get into the village so I've promised to pick up some groceries for him. He has a carer, of course. Polish woman, lovely person but old Mr Perkins doesn't trust her with his money. I think she's probably the most trustworthy carer I've met but heigh-ho, nothing as queer as some folk."

She thanked Lisa for the tea and bent down to Maria's height. "Hope to see you at the church concert, talented little girl," she said as she patted her head. Maria gazed back with a fixed smile.

Lisa was dreading the moment to tell Magdalene about the vicar's visit and the church concert. However, Maria saved her the anxiety because as soon as Magdalene came home Maria jumped into Magdalene's arms and begged her to let her go.

"Hey, what's this all about?"

Maria explained about the concert to Magdalene and was so enthused that Magdalene could not refuse. Lisa was standing in the doorway, her arms folded, watching the scene before her.

Magdalene looked up. "It will be nice," she said. "Let's go."

Maria jumped for joy.

"Lisa, mummy said that we can go. Won't that be exciting?"

"Yes, Maria darling," she said. The same sudden judder came over her and she felt perplexed as to why she felt this concert would become the catalyst of all her fears.

They decided to bring Maria's fourth birthday party a week forward so that the day of the concert would be free for Maria to play. Freddie and Peter were off to school for their first term after Christmas which prompted Lisa to meet with the head teacher. He was a local man with a local accent and he had a trimmed beard and glasses with gold frames. Mr Horwood wore a large woollen pullover over a checked shirt with a burgundy tie and brown cord trousers. He was extremely friendly and helpful and suggested to Lisa that Maria could start school at the same time as Freddie and Peter.

It all came as a bit of a shock to both Magdalene and Lisa as it dawned on them that Maria would be off to school so soon, and Lisa was particularly sad to lose her daily companion. Magdalene and Lisa wondered how Maria would settle into this new environment, but they had realised Maria's readiness and capacity to learn was so willing that it seemed the natural next step.

Magdalene was sent a school entry form in the post and as she had decided, stated that the birth certificate was lost but that she would apply for a copy. She crossed her fingers. In her experience school administrators were not always terribly efficient at chasing things up so she hoped this would be the case with Maria.

Wendy could hardly contain her excitement when she left the little cottage. She glanced back as she left to shut the latch gate, the glow from the lights inside looked warm and welcoming. The path led to a wooden porch leaden with burnished winter throngs of wisteria and ivy and roses. The front garden was neat and the drive at the side beyond the privet was hidden and safe. Snow fell softly but had grown heavier. She pulled her scarf tightly around her neck and slipped on her gloves and made her way back to the vicarage.

Once there she stoked up the log burner, filled the kettle and sorted through the post. With a cup of tea beside her she dialled some numbers into her phone.

"Hello, Henry?"

Chapter 9

Henry Pearson, Wendy's brother, had just come back from a short walk along the Cam. He liked to wend his way, following the course of the river on the opposite side of the colleges. The subject of his doctorate was on Beethoven and he knew that Beethoven had relished the sounds of the countryside and often took walks to clear his muffled soul. Henry wasn't losing his hearing like Beethoven and the thought of his deafness filled him with sorrow as he heard the murmur of river life.

He liked to get away from the din of his college house. There was forever a kaleidoscope of notes lurching though the windows, stewing up the air, swooping into his tired ears.

These days he did not do much teaching, his professorship was awash with sponsor meetings and conformity and liaisons with other professors from across the globe.

He had just got back to his rooms when he heard the phone ringing.

"Henry, Henry dear, it's sis."

Henry was longing to pour himself a large brandy but his telephone was old-fashioned and the cord was fastened to the cradle so he could not move as he listened.

He also wanted to light his fire. The room was chilly and he needed to thaw out. Dark clouds swirled past the view from his window and the noise of students below was dimmed by the dropping of the snow as they trundled away after classes.

"But Henry darling, she is a prodigy, no question. You must come to the concert dear and hear for yourself. It would be marvellous to catch up and you can stay overnight with me. I'll cook you a meal and I have some excellent brandy that a parishioner gave to me in thanks. Do please come?"

Finally, Henry agreed. He did believe his sister as it was rare for her to rave about anything really, apart from her religion. At the end of the week college would be closed for Christmas. *It would be rather lonely here*, he thought, and made travel arrangements for Kent.

The day of the Church Concert arrived and the church was packed. Helen and her family were surprised to learn that Maria was going to be playing the violin as they had no idea that she could. Lisa was accompanying her.

"It must be a version of Mozart's piece," Helen was thinking aloud.

"What?" said Tony.

"Oh, it's just that it says here that Maria is playing in the concert with Lisa. Mozart's Violin Sonata in E Minor. It says here on the programme, 'Tempo di menuetto' 5 mins. and 13 seconds. That's very precise? I didn't even know that Maria could play the violin. Mind you, she is a very bright girl and she can read fabulously well, much better than our boys."

"That's girls for you. Are her parents lesbians? I've been watching them, over there look. Yep, definitely look like a pair of dykes to me! Shall have to invite meself around darling, and I'd watch out if I were you, Helen."

Helen could not help but laugh lightly. She exclaimed that her husband was stereotyping.

"I'm sure it's all above board, darling and stop fantasising, we are in church!"

Although the village had only ever been inhabited by less than one thousand people, the church was huge. It was part of the estate which owned the land as far as the eye could see and the stately home was still lived in by the descendants of the original occupiers who were buried in flamboyant tombs at the end of the aisles. Bentley Manor was open for functions and weddings. The retired Colonel and his wife were fussing with the vicar and their huge entourage of family and friends were bustling and hustling for pews at the front.

Lisa was scarcely aware of the grandeur of the church. She had never really played in front of an audience before and she was very nervous. Maria seemed to be enjoying the limelight as she practised walking on the podium and off again. It had been built by the local carpenter especially for her so that she could be seen from the back of the church.

Helen and Tony had been so kind as to let the vicar remove their grand piano into the church for Lisa to play. It had taken some organising but the vicar's determination shone through and there it now stood, with Lisa trembling and Magdalene reassuring her at her side, being stoic.

The vaulted ceiling was high and the church was built in a sandy-coloured stone. Magdalene admired the bleakness and austerity. Every church she had been in as a catholic seemed to be weighed down by icons and the strong smell of incense. The vicar informed her that she had reserved a seat for her next to her brother, who was visiting.

The children from the school started off the concert and sang three Christmas Carols to the rapture of parents and grandparents and aunts and uncles and all...

Next was Monica who sang Mozart's 'Panis Angelicus'. It was truly awful but she smiled as the crowd applauded and delighted in her moment of fame. *People are so polite*, thought Magdalene.

Next it was Lisa and Maria's turn.

Lisa sat on the piano stool and Maria skipped onto the podium. Magdalene sensed that it was not just she who was waiting with bated breath. The church fell quiet.

Lisa nodded her head and began to play. Maria stood patiently waiting for her moment. She counted, twenty four seconds...

Maria's pre-Raphaelite curls swirled as her arm glided with the bow and her fingers danced, conjuring the sonata in ebbs and flows, in wonderment of the eventfulness of her physical reality.

The audience sat, motionless. The music reached the vaults and beyond, and the ancient walls quivered. Wendy gave a nifty side look to Henry who was slowly bewitched. She smiled and her eyes twinkled and her grey hair bobbed in its bob.

Lisa's hands fell to her sides. The crowd was hushed in anticipation. Then, like a wave, a ripple of applause swam like a swan's neck dipping first and then reaching for the sky. Lisa stood and waved her hand towards Maria. The audience rose and clapped loudly. Maria bowed her head and did a little curtsey. The she waved her hand to Lisa and the audience clapped for her too.

Henry turned to Wendy and she noticed the joy in his heart had brought him to tears.

Chapter 10

Henry decided to spend Christmas with his sister Wendy. Apart from the Christmas Carol Service at King's he wasn't really going to miss very much, he thought.

He sat on her cosy wing-backed armchair in her warm kitchen, sipping coffee that she had left on the filter machine for him and nibbled at a piece of toast and jam.

This would be the first time in ten years that the siblings had spent time together and he had to admit that he was quite looking forward to it. Wendy was a good hostess and despite her commitments to the local community, he knew that she would lay on a good Christmas for them both with all the trimmings. Anyway, he wanted to learn more about the spectacular little girl he had heard playing in the Church concert. In his view, the accompaniment was very good and quite accomplished but he thought the child was astounding and gifted; a true prodigy. In his thirty years of teaching, such rare talent had only crossed his path on no more than two occasions. Normally, child prodigies didn't come to him until later in their careers. Gaining a place at his college, which was part of the University of Cambridge, was difficult for candidates. He sighed to himself and rephrased that sentence in his head, it was difficult, he thought, but now candidates would mostly be judged on whether they could pay the fees or not. A lot of his students were from overseas. As he grew older he found the language barrier harder to overcome and his patience was tiring. He knew he should be considering his retirement but somehow he needed to be pushed to do it. He felt certain that this would happen soon. New blood was coming through the ranks at college; he didn't mind, he was ready. But this girl? Was she one last opportunity to raise his excitement again, one last chance to share some limelight? Could she bring to him one last round of glory in the concerto circuit?

Sometimes Henry wondered whether God was having a joke by blessing such young people and often he had witnessed how badly their gifts were managed. Puberty, drugs, sex and rock and roll left their indelible mark like a birth mark on the meek. *How unfair*, he thought. Some came through and went on to successful careers by securing fabulous recording deals and some became celebrities. He had even heard of one American pianist who had launched his own aftershave brand, who'd have thought?

In his own way he was an excellent musician but he had always known that he had lacked the spark to fire him like a heavenly bolt across the bows of thundering composition. The natural musicality of conjuring sublime notes one after the other had never come to him. This led him to wonder if little Maria could read music, or if she played by rote? *Soon,* he thought, *I will find out.*

This girl, Henry thought again, *she is different. Probably she is only four or five? She seemed very small up there on the podium.* He would question Wendy when she got back from her litany of parishioner visits. He felt a glad tiding course through his veins and he allowed himself a satisfied expression as he envisaged the little girl playing at the Royal Albert Hall whilst he watched in acknowledgement in his role of bringing her to that point in time. His last summer time.

Wendy came home, all rosy cheeked, bringing with her a Tupperware box filled with cakes and mince pies.

She kissed him lightly on the cheek.

"It's just so lovely to come home knowing that you are here, dear."

Wendy cooked lunch and the pair retired to the sitting room to watch the Christmas Carol Concert on the BBC from King's College, Cambridge.

The Christmas period carried on as normal for Lisa, Magdalene and Maria. Maria had woken on Christmas morning to a huge pillow case crammed with toys and treats. Lisa prepared a light breakfast as Magdalene stuffed the turkey and opened a bottle of bubbly which she drank mostly to herself, her time being consumed with preparing vegetables, side dishes and pigs in blankets. Magdalene had a huge appetite and wolfed down pieces of carrot and celery as she went along.

Lisa and Maria set the table and put Christmas pop songs on the Hi-Fi, singing along happily as Maria laid out knives and forks and spoons and Lisa showed her how to make lily pads out of paper napkins.

After lunch each person opened their presents from under the tree. Maria was thrilled to find that both Freddie and Peter had given her a present. It was a board game called, 'Battleships'. We can play that later, Lisa had told her.

Magdalene gave to Lisa a white crystal necklace and bracelet to match. On the clasp of the bracelet was engraved an old Irish blessing, '*May the road rise to meet you. May the wind be always at your back. May the sun shine warm upon your face; the rains fall soft upon your fields and until we meet again, may God hold you in the hollow of his hand.*'

"It's gorgeous and thoughtful," said Lisa. "But a little sad, I hope that we are not going to be parted?"

"It's just an old Irish blessing and I wish you to have all of those things. Have you looked at the clasp on the necklace?" Magdalene asked.

Lisa took the necklace and etched on the clasp was written, '*Like the Ladies of Llangollen.*'

'Like the Ladies of Llangollen,' Lisa read it out.

"Who are they?" asked Maria. "Do I know them?"

"Yes, in a way, you do," Magdalene explained. "The Ladies of Llangollen are very similar to me and Lisa."

Maria quickly became disinterested as she anticipated the next gift.

This was a present from Lisa to Magdalene. Unwrapping shades of cool mint wrapping paper, Magdalene found inside some gold tissue wrap and inside that was a small jewellery box. She opened it cautiously and as she did Lisa fell to one knee.

"Marry me, Mags, please?"

Planning the wedding was a great distraction for Lisa who missed Maria terribly when she took her off to school. Maria had taken everything in her stride and was full of glee to learn that she would spend her school days with Freddie and Peter.

Over the New Year Lisa used the internet to find friendly 'Civil Partnership' locations. She pored over magazines and created a 'Mood Board' for colour themes for her and Magdalene. Maria, of course, would be bridesmaid.

It would be a small affair, and as Lisa wrote out the invitations, she realised that after inviting the Chads she could not think of who else to ask. Freddie and Peter made up the Chad foursome and she decided to ask Helen and Tony to be their witnesses. Lisa understood that she was going to a lot of trouble for such a tiny event but encouraged herself by chatting endlessly to Magdalene and reminding Magdalene that she had never been married before and how special this day was to her.

She missed Maria so much that it was nice to fill her time in by becoming the supreme wedding planner. Rings, outfits, flowers, venue, reception and meal choices - she had organised it all. The date was April 11th and she hoped that spring would be at its fullest. She picked a medieval manor house that could deliver the whole package and she had booked the honeymoon suite for an overnight stay, as Helen had offered to take Maria home with her for the night. Lisa had chosen Bentley Hall, a mere mile away, and she was surprisingly pleased to learn that lots of same sex couples held ceremonies there. *How enlightened of the Colonel,* she thought.

Meanwhile, Henry had returned to Cambridge and handed in his notice. During his time with Wendy over Christmas she had agreed that he could go and live with her. Wendy realised that Henry was hanging on to his professorship like flies to jam because he would find it hard to let it all go. After all, he had worked so very hard to achieve his status and neither sibling had received much support from their parents. Each had spent their youth in boarding schools and went on to Oxbridge and their paths had taken directions that neither had argued against.

In many ways Cambridge had been all-consuming for Henry who had never married, although he had some flings and had been hurt romantically, from which he had never seemed to recover. Wendy told herself to be thankful that she now had the company of dear Henry to look forward to.

February half-term week came and Henry packed up a few things to visit Wendy. He wasn't officially moving in until the end of the summer term, but as he was travelling up it made sense to him to bring some clothes and antiquities that he had collected over the years. His college didn't actually have a half term, mainly down to the extra cost to students from overseas who simply did not want to fly off to visit family for a few short days, but other members of staff, keen to be seen to be keen, kindly volunteered to cover for him.

Wendy had assigned to him a large bedroom at the back of the house. It had a firm double bed with a feather mattress and old-fashioned wooden furniture that smelled of mothballs. Wendy was allowed to stay in the Vicarage until she died. *I hope I go first, in that case then,* he was thinking as he placed a bust of Beethoven on the mantel.

As he did so, Wendy came in.

"No Henry dear, no need to hide Beethoven up here. Bring him down to the sitting room and he can sit on the mantel where we can both marvel, hmm?" As she spoke she swept up the bust. Henry watched nervously as she took it downstairs.

I'll have to get used to that, he thought. *Wendy always was a bit bossy,* he remembered.

Over supper Henry broached the subject of the little girl and was pleased to find that Wendy was a very willing participant about filling him in on all her gossip.

"I think they are lesbians, Henry and..." not pausing for breath, she went on, "actually my suspicions are confirmed as I've heard they are having a Civil Partnership in the spring up at Bentley Manor."

"Shame you never married, Wends," Henry replied with a subtle inference that hinted he had surmised that Wendy's inclinations were not much different from the two women she was now happy to be gossiping about.

Wendy ignored him and continued. She told him that the little girl was named Maria (he sighed, he already knew this) and it was she - and that Henry was always to remember this - that it was she who had first heard her playing through the window. She rattled on, informing Henry that it may be important to remember that one day as she was sure that Maria was going to be famous and it was she, Wendy Pearson, who had discovered her.

Henry had by now switched off as his mind was busily hatching a plan to meet with Maria and her lesbian mothers.

At the concert Lisa had picked up some clients and a few requests to tune pianos, mostly uprights but she was happy to comply as this could lead to more lessons. This included the Colonel whom she thought had flirted with her and he had amused Magdalene and Lisa at the Church. He too had a grand piano which stood in a grand function room. There were seats in rows covered in white fabric with cerulean ribbons and there were flower holders all around, awaiting decorations. Lisa loved the splendour of this room and imagined when she and Mags would be standing in it, holding hands together, declaring their love for one another.

She had planned the service colour scheme to match the colours of this room, and the bouquets would be made up of cornflowers and flowers of pastel pinks and purples as if they had just been plucked from a country meadow.

She was jolted out of her daydream by the voice of Henry. Wendy had introduced them at the concert and she remembered his blue eyes.

"So sorry to disturb you. I was just calling in for a drink and I heard you tuning the piano. Would you care to join me?"

Lisa hesitated and looked at her watch. Two o'clock. She had an hour and a half before she needed to collect Maria.

"Why not?" she said, hoping that Wendy's brother wasn't looking for a romance.

She joined him at the bar and he ordered them both a good quality red wine, she noticed. He had also ordered some savouries to munch as they sat rather awkwardly on the worn Georgian chairs.

Henry began the conversation. He focused on Lisa's playing at the concert and flattered her. It was his tactic to lure her into talking about Maria. He had some experience of women and engaged Lisa whilst his blue eyes gleamed, surveying her slim body. Lisa liked him. She had never really chatted with anyone as clever as he obviously was, and he impressed her with his silent modesty. He talked about Beethoven and the time slipped by before she realised but she wanted more of him.

Lisa liked his laugh which was contagious and before long Henry had ordered another glass of wine.

She checked her watch.

"Oh Lordy!" she exclaimed. "It's 3 o'clock. Sorry, must dash as I need to pick up Maria from the Chads'."

"Do you need a lift?"

"No, I've got my bike thanks."

"I'm here again tomorrow if you'd like to join me?"

Lisa was heading off towards the door but she turned and called back.

"Yes, lovely, just need to check my diary."

That evening when Magdalene was home and the three females tucked into supper, Lisa studied her partner. Things had changed between them as they had settled into their routine of domesticity but she still felt aroused by the thought of Magdalene's touch and the comforting feeling of settling her head between her abundant breasts. Magdalene was on one of her never-ending diets, trying to shed a few pounds for the ceremony, but as ever Lisa watched her spoon gigantic mouthfuls of the delicious pasta into her sexy mouth between her even white teeth. *Maria could be her daughter* she thought as she watched the pair. They are very similar and she observed Maria's mannerisms which reflected those of her adopted mother. A thought dashed across her mind about the birth certificate but it was easily six weeks since Maria had started school and no correspondence or mention of it had come up. *Perhaps Magdalene was right about that*, she thought.

Lisa wished that she could be as content as Magdalene about Maria's circumstances but she always had a nagging doubt at the back of her mind, even though she tried hard to sweep it away. She continually feared that she and Mags would be found out one day. Tonight, she decided that she wasn't going to think about it and she twizzled her bracelet with the shiny crystals. She was looking forward to meeting with the professor again tomorrow and for now she would keep it to herself.

Lisa rode her bicycle up to Bentley Manor and made for the bar where Henry was waiting. He broadly smiled as she came in and she noticed a few local people that she did not know but knew by sight were seated around enjoying a substantial bar meal. She smiled and nodded at them as she joined Henry at the bar.

She had guessed that he was perhaps around fifty five years of age but he held himself in the manner of someone younger and she wondered what he did to keep fit. He was quite well-toned for his age and she concluded he was vain. Henry was a bit of an enigma, she thought, as on the one hand he seemed liked a doting old Professor of Music and yet on another level there was some mischief and fun and youth about him. He gestured for her to sit in the seats where they had sat yesterday, facing the bar yet inconspicuously private where no one would overhear their conversation. He brought over two glasses and with them a bottle of the deep red wine, the same wine as yesterday, she noticed. *Oh good,* she thought.

He was dressed casually with an open check shirt and paisley silk cravat. She was curious if he wore this to cover his old wrinkled neck but he looked stylish in his chinos and plentiful sleeked black hair streaked with grey.

It wasn't long before Henry enticed Lisa into speaking about Maria.

The red wine made Lisa feel giddy and she devoured the crisps and nuts and olives in an attempt to soak it up. Henry had turned intimately beside her and had taken some strands of Lisa's blonde hair between his fingers, twisting them as he spoke, nursing and coaxing her to tell him more about Maria. Lisa hadn't noticed. Thankfully, it was so engrained in Lisa's mind not to discuss the finer points about Maria's true heritage that she did not disclose any details. She confirmed to him that Maria could sight-read music and that she had been playing the piano since she could walk.

Henry had responded with words such as, 'Outstanding' and 'Brilliant'. He had smothered Lisa with compliments about her teaching skills and implied that he was simply offering to help Lisa bring on this gifted child that she guarded so well.

"After all," he said. "We are both talented musicians with lots in common, Lisa, I think we can help each other out here." When it was almost time to leave to pick up Maria from the Chads, Lisa had agreed with Henry that she would bring Maria tomorrow so that he could hear her play on the grand piano in the function room.

Chapter 11

Henry left Kent with no doubt in his mind about the sequence of actions he was about to undertake. He was 'blown away' by Maria. Her playing, her sight-reading, her brightness and her wisdom. *There is something unique about her*, he thought. Oh no, not just that she was a brilliant and gifted musician, but something else he couldn't put his finger on.

He made an appointment with the Chancellor who agreed to release Henry earlier after the Easter break. Richard Spinks had been hankering for a promotion at Trinity for a while and was charming his way around the music faculty with knightly endeavour, so Henry's leaving and replacement was no loss to the faculty. This meant that Henry could depart from his old world and head out to his new one.

Next, he searched for his diary of contacts and looked up 'M' for Micklethwaite. Percy Micklethwaite was scrawled in Henry's doctor-like handwriting and next to it was his mobile number.

Meanwhile Lisa and Magdalene lived their life in their Kentish village and luxuriated in their tempered zone of day-to-day bliss.

Magdalene had become anxious one day when she received a letter from the school, thinking it may be about the birth certificate. It was from the nice Head Teacher Lisa had told her about, asking if he could have permission for Maria to be photographed in their 'Easter Bonnet Parade'. Instantly she realised that it was a standard letter which had gone out to all parents. She signed the returned slip at the bottom of the letter with some satisfaction, *Magdalene Amari* and placed it inside Maria's school bag.

Maria was excited about the forthcoming events. Lisa had taken her into Tunbridge Wells to try on some bridesmaids dresses and Maria felt dressed up like a princess. Lisa ordered a wide cerulean ribbon to go around the waist of her cream dress and she watched as the assistant tied it swiftly into a large bow.

Maria was ecstatic about the Easter Bonnet Parade and felt sure that her entry would win. She and Lisa spent the blustery March evenings sewing ribbons and felt rabbits onto an old straw hat of Magdalene's, and they made flower petals out of tissue paper to decorate it.

In Lisa's Civil Partnership planner file she was adeptly ticking off tasks as the day drew near. Easter fell early and the parade would be held in the Church the Sunday before their wedding, which fell on a Wednesday.

Maria's teacher, Miss Finchfield, had practised their line-up with the children and found Maria bossing the twins, who seemed to be under her spell as they gladly gave in to her demands. *Those three are more like triplets,* she thought, as they were inseparable. Miss Finchfield, who wore a bright platinum sparkling engagement ring and was slim and petite with long red hair held in an Alice band, was grateful for the bright girl in her classroom. Maria would help the twins with their reading and when tested she had shown that her reading age was around nine years, a good three or four years above her actual age. She was good at maths too and her classroom was adorned by diagrams and graphs that Maria had produced on the computer. Miss Finchfield felt a bit outdone at times by Maria, who would rise up to the challenge at the next computing level beyond her own skills and Maria would often chastise Miss Finchfield when she did not use the shortcuts on the computer. Maria would inform her that it would save her a lot of work and time if she would just brush up. Annoyingly,

Maria would be right but despite Maria's arrogance Miss Finchfield liked her. She found her bright and happy but mysteriously very wise for a girl her age. She had questioned Maria when she found her talking to her imaginary friend but when Maria replied that he was helping her with her maths she did not object. Children were a funny lot, and for all their pretentions and habits they were only children after all, she often thought. She liked Maria's nanny and she wondered whether to broach the subject of Maria's imaginary friend with her but gathered that she probably already knew. Maria was such a happy and loving girl she conceded to let the matter go. She hadn't met her mother yet and supposed she would attend the Easter bonnet festival.

Magdalene had holiday from work for the whole of the Easter break. She eagerly looked forward to the ceremony and on the Friday night, when she managed to get home early, she and Lisa went to bed to make love. Caressing Lisa's languorous body she contemplated their relationship and how things had moved on since those quiet days in her Hampstead garden.

Lisa was bursting to tell Magdalene about the concert performance that she had granted to Henry but considered that this would be best left until after the ceremony.

Henry had arranged for Maria to play the second week of the Easter break at a small concert hall in Tonbridge. The hall was at one of the many public schools where Henry had connections with the organiser, and he felt that it would make a fine and welcome start to Maria's career. Lisa could not recall exactly what she had concurred with Henry about Maria's career but the date, place and time had stuck in her mind. She had secretly been tutoring Maria the new piece she was learning in three movements, Mozart's Piano Sonata No.11 in A Major. K33-1, Andante Grazioso.

As Magdalene stroked Lisa's tummy she felt hugely guilty of keeping this secret from Magdalene. It did not sit well with her, especially at this time of binding in their relationship. She would tell her after the honeymoon night. It would be something for them both to look forward to. She just prayed that Mags wouldn't be angry.

March blew itself out and April rolled in with a modest sprouting of bluebells, and the last of the daffodils gave way to proud tulips nodding in cool rainy breezes that showered the county of Kent.

Maria and the twins were beside themselves hopping and dancing about beneath the vaults of the great church in readiness for their grand Easter Bonnet Parade. The vicar was in her pulpit announcing the judges, Henry, the Colonel and the local President of the WI.

"Hi, Helen," Magdalene said. Magdalene was adjusting the tie under Maria's bonnet, who was complaining that it was too tight. She was surrounded by all of her year who were jostling for places in the line, shouting at one another to stand in the right spot.

"God this is madness, isn't it?" Her Irish accent was pleasant but affirmative.

"Sure is," said Helen. "Where's Lisa?"

"Over there with Miss Finchfield. I'll come over with you as I need to meet her."

"Haven't you met her yet?"

"No – first time for everything!"

"She's very nice, Magdalene, and she loves Maria. You should visit her classroom. The walls are covered in Maria's work. You must be very proud?"

"I am, I will," responded Magdalene, feeling slightly uncomfortable that she hadn't done so already. *What sort of mother am I?* she thought.

Miss Finchfield shook Magdalene's hand over the top of a skinny boy who still looked tiny in his tall hat.

"And this is Mr Horwood, the Head," she said as she introduced the man wearing a large knitted jumper which had a picture of a chicken on the front.

Magdalene nodded to him.

"I'll be just off to my seat then, before you start," she said, kissing Maria on the cheek.

"Don't forget, it's not all about the winning but taking part," she told Maria.

Maria looked startled.

"No mummy, Mo, Mo says I am bound to win."

Magdalene had returned to her seat as the children paraded up and down the aisle like mice, tiptoeing and grinning toothless smiles at relatives and friends, touching their bonnets for reassurance.

She was seated next to Henry who said 'Hello' and 'How are you?'

They really couldn't talk very much as the children were making a din, but at the end he sought Magdalene out at the refreshment table.

"You must be very proud of Maria," he said.

"More than I can say, or ever will be able to," she replied.

"Lisa is doing such a great job with her musical capabilities. You must be looking forward to the upcoming concert in Tonbridge? Very exciting," he smiled, making sure it was one of his most charming.

"Sorry? Concert in Tonbridge?"

Ah, Henry guessed that Lisa hadn't shared their secret. This was delicate but he proceeded.

"Totally down to me. I'm afraid I got your nanny a bit tiddly and she agreed for Maria to appear at a concert an old acquaintance of mine is holding the week after your ceremony. Don't blame Lisa, it's all my doing. Your daughter has such a talent you know, Magdalene. I hope I can call you Magdalene? She obviously gets it from her mother. Your hair is pretty amazing, I can see where Maria gets that from. And those pretty freckles, how delightful. Do you play anything yourself?"

Magdalene was stunned and inside her head she was imagining herself punching this sickeningly charming old git.

"Yes, of course I know all about it" she uttered with some contempt. "See you there." She turned quickly to find Lisa who was chatting with Helen and Tony with the usual mayhem of twins and Maria dashing between legs, up and over the old pews, much to the dismay of the vicar.

Magdalene gulped the vinegary wine on offer and then downed another two glasses with the same vigour.

She smiled politely at Lisa and grabbed hold of her arm.

"Lisa, darling nanny, come along, it's getting late and we need all our beauty sleep for Wednesday."

"Fine Magdalene, bye Helen, bye Tony, bye twins, see you on Wednesday?"

Outside the church, Lisa stopped Magdalene.

"What was that urgent exit all about?" she asked.

"You tell me! I think you've got something to tell me about that new piece Maria's been rehearsing, and why?"

Lisa could not help but feel a little put out at Magdalene's manner as she very much felt that she was Maria's mother too. She reminded Magdalene that it was only a pretention to the outside world that she was Maria's nanny.

"Yes, but for God's sake Lisa, you should have told me."

"I was going to but what with all the arrangements for our ceremony, I just couldn't find the right time."

Magdalene was gripping Maria's hand as she skipped along beside her.

"Maria, would you like to play in this concert that you have been rehearsing for?"

Maria was very affirmative in her response as she smiled her angelic smile up at Magdalene.

"OK, this time you can do it, but no more secrets. Don't keep any secrets from mummy. And that goes for you too, Lisa."

Lisa smiled and kissed Magdalene on the cheek.

"Well, after the ceremony it gives us something new to look forward to, oh come on Mags, cheer up, it will be fun. Our bright little star shining on the stage and Maria is desperate to do it. She has an amazing talent. No, not talent, it's a gift from God and we should not hide it away. Henry is just bedazzled by her and he should know, with his experience, he says that he has never, in his life time, come across such ability."

"It's just that I am worried, Leese," she dropped her voice, "What if we get found out?"

"Well, I guess that's the risk we will have to take but no matter what *we* do, we won't be able to hide Maria from the world." Lisa felt uneasy at Magdalene's unusual shake of confidence.

Maria was still excited about winning the Easter Bonnet Parade and when they arrived home she was allowed to play on the piano for a while to calm her. She was chatting to Mo, Mo telling him all about her evening. After a while Lisa managed to coax her into bed.

Snuggled up together that night, Magdalene kissed Lisa gently.

"Only a few more days and we two will be as one."

"I know," replied Lisa. "Like the Ladies of Llangollen."

Chapter 12

The day of their ceremony arrived with brisk golden sunshine. Blossom trees in scented yellow and pinks lined the pretty lanes. At Rose Cottage there was a buzz and hive of activity as the females in the household prepared themselves for their big day. Dresses were ironed, hair was put up, make-up applied and posies arranged.

Lisa had arranged for a pony and trap to take them up to Bentley Manor, and as they set off in their Empire line dresses and cerulean ribbons, the scene could be mistaken for characters from a Jane Austen novel. However, there was no male groom for any woman present to esteem.

The ceremony was a short affair and lasted for about thirty minutes. Magdalene's dress on her bosom showed a large amount of cleavage and as she held hands with Lisa, as they walked slowly past the empty chairs to meet the registrar, Henry could not help but notice how her breasts wobbled, and he had a vision of holding his head between them. He had made an offer to Lisa to switch on the CD as they walked up to meet the Registrar and Lisa had accepted. *Bloody shame they're lezzers,* he thought to himself. He turned on the music, 'Hush Sweet Lover' by KD Lang as the pair entered the room together, with Maria hopping and dancing along behind. She quickly became his focus of attention. His thoughts were greedy as he gazed at the girl with such promise. *My glory exists just there,* he thought. *Within that child with the haunting eyes.* He faded out the music when the women arrived at the table where the registrar stood waiting.

During the signing of the Register Lisa had chosen the Mozart Piano Sonata that Maria had been practising so eagerly and Henry obliged by replacing the original CD. Helen and Tony were witnesses and for once the twins sat quietly. Each was wide-eyed as they watched Maria, and each in their own mind thought she looked beautiful.

Afterwards, there was a three-course meal and Magdalene made a toast which was brief: "We may be made in the image of God, but I've never seen him and I am sure if I did he wouldn't be a man but a woman, as apparently we are the gender that can multi-task and God certainly got up to a lot of multi-tasking."

Helen and Tony laughed and Henry laughed too, despite himself.

She went on: "I would just like to give thanks to my striking bride and to our gorgeous bridesmaid. May we all live long and happy together."

Helen, Tony, Henry and the twins echoed her last words and Magdalene popped open a bottle of expensive champagne.

Helen and Tony left with Maria and the twins for the night, wishing the couple well.

Henry lingered for a while, sedated by the good food and wine.

"I'll need to come and visit you both, to help Maria prepare for next week," he said.

"I've got something for you," he said handing over a glossy brochure.

There on the front was a picture of Maria sat at a piano with the words, 'A fantastic evening of classical music played by promising young artists of our time. Not to be missed!"

He must have taken that photograph of Maria here that day, thought Lisa. I wish he had told me.

Magdalene took the brochure and smiled at Henry.

"That's fab Henry. Now, Lisa and I have our honeymoon to look forward to."

Henry took the hint and left.

Chapter 13

Percy Micklethwaite was waiting anxiously at the main entrance to the imposing Victorian hall. He was concerned as he had put all his eggs in one basket for this evening. He just hoped that this little girl was as good as Henry had made out. He was pleased that the concert was a sell-out, but he really did not want any bad reviews as his reputation would not stand it.

Henry arrived with two women. One woman was very plump, he noticed, the other slim and pretty. *Jack Sprat shall eat no fat and so on...,* he thought to himself.

He spied the little girl. Pretty and freckled with the most deep and soft eyes he thought he had ever seen. They seem to expose wisdom of years beyond her age. He was rather transfixed, and then he heard Henry speak.

"Percy, Percy old boy. Meet Magdalene Amari, Maria's mother, and this is her partner, Lisa Smith. And this little sweet pea here is Maria."

Everyone shook hands and Percy escorted the group behind the curtained stage where a grand piano sat, and next to it, a music stand ready for the other children who would be playing clarinet, violin and trumpet that evening.

Magdalene and Lisa knew from the programme that Maria would be the last performer. They came prepared with snacks and drinks and games to amuse Maria whilst she waited her turn.

Maria was fascinated by the other boys and girls performing and sat patiently in the wings. Occasionally she would flinch if a wrong note was played but the audience didn't seem to notice. *Or,* perhaps Maria thought, *they just don't mind like Mo, Mo minds.*

Lisa had bought Maria a crimson velvet dress and her hair was left long with ringlets tucked into a neat black velvet ribbon. She wore black tights and black patent shoes which attracted the light from the spots. Maria, so tiny and looking so vulnerable, entered the stage.

She took a confident bow and sat herself comfortably on the piano stool. There was a hush in the room and Lisa and Magdalene gripped each other in anticipation. Henry had been to their house every day since the day after their ceremony and Maria had rehearsed for at least five hours a day. She never complained. Henry had noticed that she would stop from time to time and look into the middle distance as if she was acknowledging someone else in the room. It seemed to him to be unearthly as he watched her engage in conversation with someone who was not there. Tingles had run down his spine and Lisa happened to come in at one point. Noticing Henry's face, which looked a little frightened, she watched Maria in her ritual of speaking with 'Mo, Mo'. She reassured Henry, stating that Maria was simply chatting with her imaginary friend.

Henry accepted this fact with grace and Lisa was pleased as she did not want Henry to start digging any deeper.

In the hall, Maria's straight back let loose her magic hands and she played the Mozart Piano Sonata No.11 adeptly, profoundly and with wonder.

When she finished there was no sound except for the last waft of the last note that curled in the air like a cloud.

Then suddenly the audience were on their feet, applauding. Maria heard shouts of 'Bravo, Bravo.' Percy Micklethwaite came on stage and gave Maria a bouquet of red roses. He was grinning from ear to ear. *Bloody bugger,* he thought of Henry. *Trust him to be the one to spot this child.* There was no doubt in his mind that she was the best child prodigy that he had ever heard.

Due to Maria's resounding success Henry offered to take Magdalene, Lisa and Maria out to dinner.

Maria's eyes were glowing and her cheeks were flushed. She had enjoyed the applause which went on for ages and she had realised that her playing had been the best of the night. Other than that, she seemed nonplussed by the event.

Percy managed to invite himself along to dinner as he wanted to discuss the 'BBC Young Musician of the Year' which was open to young people like Maria whom, he thought, and told the waiting group, was an excellent candidate.

Lisa and Magdalene were overwhelmed by the attention Maria was being given. Some of the other children looked upon her with a high degree of jealousy but Maria did not seem to notice.

Maria did not want to go out for dinner. All she wished for was to be home to see 'Mo, Mo' and tell him all about her outstanding performance. *He will be so proud of me,* she thought. To Maria, the only praise she craved was his.

It was agreed over dinner by Henry and Percy that Maria should enter for the 'BBC Young Musician of the Year'. Because Maria was sitting sulkily and by the fact that she looked so tired, Magdalene realised that she was conveniently submitting to Henry and Percy's wishes. She was not in the mood to sit there any longer to hear the pair tweeting like a couple of clucking hens and she agreed to their demands so that the Amari household could make a quick getaway.

There had just been a 'Young Musician of the Year' award which Maria missed, so Henry and Lisa began schooling Maria in earnest for the following year. Over the eleven months that followed Maria practised two pieces, Mozart's Piano Sonata No. 16 in C Major and Mozart's Piano Concerto No.21 in C Major K467 for piano and orchestra. With the wonders of technology, Henry devised the orchestral pieces on the computer so that Maria could become accustomed to the sounds before he had an opportunity for her to practice with the real thing. He contacted his old college and arranged to take Maria regularly to play with the student orchestra who were pleased to support the young genius.

Somehow the group settled into the routine of school runs, high days and holidays and another happy and peaceful Christmas at 'Rose Cottage'.

Maria steadily grew. She had long spindly legs and by now her hair had grown beyond her middle back. She was tested at school and in everything she attained the score of a child in advance of her years, by at least five years. That was everything except music, of course, where there was not an exam in existence to test her, as Maria surpassed them all. She was already beyond Grade 8 in piano. She wasn't so keen on the violin and yet she had managed to pass Grade 5 quite easily. She had a strong voice as well, and she often hummed along as she played.

That year, her relationship with Mo, Mo became more intense. Maria started to chat with him at the table, in bed at night and she had even persuaded the twins to include Mo, Mo in all their games.

Lisa and Magdalene had become accustomed to Maria's growing imagination and included Mo, Mo in their daily routines. Henry put it down to an outlet, as no one person, he thought, could contain so much talent without a distraction. He didn't like being on his own in the room with Maria when she invited Mo, Mo's comments. He thought it was spooky and unnatural. Quite frankly, at times, this child gave him the creeps, but he could never fathom out why.

Chapter 14

Henry and Lisa were more than confident that Maria was prepared for the BBC competition. Inside, Henry was burning with desire as he envisioned being interviewed by a BBC commentator and being recognised for his great work with Maria Amari. He heard the words in his head, 'So, Henry Pearson, when did you first come across Maria? What was your first impression? Did you expect her to rise so gallantly to this occasion?' She would be the youngest contestant ever. He had practised in his head the words that he would use to respond. The best part would be when he would exclaim, 'Maria Amari is *my* protégé.'

Events took a turn for the unexpected when Henry informed Lisa that the contest for this year was in Prague. This bombshell made Lisa feel sick and she had to excuse herself to go to the bathroom. She knew what this meant. Maria could not go. How would she explain to Maria, Henry, all the people involved, that there was no way on earth that Maria Amari would own a passport and fly to Prague? Why hadn't Henry mentioned this to her before?

She checked herself in the mirror and returned to Henry in the sitting room. The lesson had finished, and Maria was finishing off a Lego build that she had started with the twins. She felt engulfed by the bombshell but took a deep breath.

"Sorry, Henry, I think I ate something dodgy for lunch. Now what were you saying about Prague?"

It was a bleak February evening on Valentine's night when Magdalene returned home. The miserable sky was threatening rain as the clouds heaved indignantly across the torrid sky. She held a bunch of red roses and a box of hand-made chocolates. She was tired, it had been a long day and someone had thrown themselves across the train track, holding up the Jubilee line so home-going Londoners were forced to find other means of travel.

Work was going well. She had been promoted to Manager of her department and she now controlled a team of six. It was not too difficult as they were mainly geeks and relished the challenges she gave to them. She never discussed her home life, but on odd occasions alluded to Maria, but never mentioned Lisa by name, only stating that she had done this or that at the weekend with her partner.

The heterosexuals in the office tended to relate all their happenings on a Monday morning. People seemed to assume that her partner was male. Half of the trouble was that she couldn't be bothered to explain. She didn't mind people knowing that she was a lesbian. The heterosexuals were constantly on mobile phones texting a lover, a boyfriend, a wife or husband discussing what was for dinner and other tedious matters. Magdalene never did any of those things and kept herself to herself. Now and then the team would meet up on a Friday for after work drinks and she went along thinking it was nice to be social. As their manager, she would leave early, not wishing to impose and she would say that she had to get back to Maria. Tonight was such an evening. If she hadn't stayed for drinks she would have been home ages ago. *Never mind,* she thought. It's Valentine's Day, and she suspected that Lisa was going to cook a delicious romantic meal for the pair, scurrying Maria off to bed early.

Almost as soon as she had opened the door Lisa pounced on her.

"Magdalene, Magdalene," she was crying. "What are we to do? What are we to do...?"

The two women talked through the night, the chocolates and roses discarded. What were they to do?

"She can't go," Magdalene said. "There is no way we can get a passport for her. We'll just have to play along with Henry and pretend that she has become ill nearer the time, and that she is too ill to travel."

"Maria will be devastated," Lisa said.

"Not as much as we will be, Leese. I can't bear to imagine what might happen. This is our story and we will have to stick to it."

So, this is what the women agreed, and Maria, oblivious to her dilemma, continued to master the music scores that Henry meticulously went through with her, and she travelled to Cambridge to practice with the adoring students. Henry was a good tutor, stern and rigid in the context of her musicality but he coaxed and encouraged Maria. The students were amazed at her ability and would discuss her outstanding gift at great length in the local bars and cafés.

A student girl of Russian descent exclaimed that; 'it's as if Mozart is in her mind and hands, playing the piece as if she is possessed by him.'

The other students agreed and said this could be the only possible explanation and from there on between them referred to Maria as the 'Ghost'.

Henry noticed that Lisa had dark circles under her eyes. Her glasses seem to emphasise them.

One day, a month before the competition was due, he enquired after Lisa's health. She told him that everything was fine and that she was just tired and had a lot of work on just lately.

Henry was uneasy. He did not want anything to scupper his plans.

"Just thought Lisa, your passports are all up-to-date aren't they? Better check mine after me saying that. I took the liberty of typing up a schedule for the stay in Prague. Hotel, flight numbers and so on. I'm becoming quite the administrator in my retirement!"

Lisa fixed her eyes on Henry. Staring at him but not really registering his face. Her mind was racing.

"Yes, everything in order of course, Henry," she said cheerily and offered him a cup of tea. Henry's relief was palpable.

Both Magdalene and Lisa looked worn out as the days towards the competition grew near. Lisa lost weight and Magdalene drank more wine. Both women found it hard to keep up the pretence to Maria, each feeling the pain that they would cause her by keeping her at home. They dared not even consider Henry's wrath, and Magdalene damned and cursed the day they had ever met him. How had she let things get so out of control? This was not what she had plotted. She watched Maria develop her skills and her mastery of the music was unquestionable. It was such a shame and a deep pity that she could not go to Prague. For the first time, for a long time, she prayed. She prayed that the competition would be in the UK next year and Maria could take part in that one. It was of little commiseration, but it may help ease the pain.

Maria was excitable. She could not sit still for a minute and Lisa arranged lots of play-dates with the twins to keep her occupied. Her heart ached. She was dreading giving the news. She and Magdalene had decided that they would put Maria to bed the day before the flight. In the night Lisa would take her temperature, exclaiming it was high and say that Maria was definitely coming down with something. It was going to be difficult to convince Maria. Lisa hoped that she would not work out their ruse but it was, after all it seemed to her, the only solution. Magdalene would handle Henry and inform him by phone the day they were all due to fly out to Prague.

As it happened the twins came down with a virus and Lisa put Maria to bed the eve of the flight and whispered that she hoped Maria hadn't caught it. Magdalene and Lisa went to her in the night with a cold flannel and woke her.

"Maria darling," said Magdalene. "You've been restless and woke me and Lisa, you were crying out. Open your mouth sweetie, for Lisa to take your temperature."

Maria, half asleep and confused, obeyed. She didn't feel hot and she had been dreaming of standing on the stage receiving tumultuous applause as she ended her performance. Mo, Mo had told her that she would win the competition. She had also dreamed of flying on a plane. In the summer months she and the twins would lie on the grass and watch the vapour trails in the sky. It was important to show off to one another their geography knowledge as they called out the names of the countries the planes were cruising to. Surprisingly, it wasn't Maria who won these games but Freddie. He would yell out what seemed to Maria exotic names: India, Africa, Malaysia and the Seychelles. One day he had shouted 'Austria' and Maria haughtily informed Freddie that it wasn't fair as this was her favourite country as it was Mo, Mo's country and only she could shout its name. Freddie, with his usual aplomb, shrugged his shoulders.

"Well, you're never going to go there," he said.

"I so will," replied Maria. Just you wait, Freddie, I am going to all the countries of this world, and anyway, I'm going to Prague and you're not."

Freddie knew better than to argue with Maria. He rolled over and started tickling her tummy. She roared with glee and tickled him back until he got up and ran away and she and Peter chased him around the garden.

Maria snapped out of her thought bubble as Lisa put a cold flannel on her forehead. Suddenly, the realisation of what was happening dawned on Maria. She took the flannel and flung it across her pink princess bedroom.

"I'm not sick, I'm not sick!" she yelled.

"There, there, dear," said Magdalene, putting her arms around her. "You may not feel sick right now but your temperature is soaring, you are definitely coming down with something. You probably caught it from the twins."

She sat upright, jolted by the implications of being sick.

"What about Prague, mummy?"

"Let's see how you are tomorrow morning. Now put this flannel back on your forehead and try and get some rest. I'll sit with you until you fall asleep."

But Maria could not sleep. When the sun began to stream through her window she observed Magdalene lolling with her chin hanging down as she snored quietly in the white wicker chair. She felt rotten. *There's more to this*, she thought. At her young age she didn't know what it was but in that moment she knew she wasn't going to Prague.

Lisa brought her some toast, jam and juice for breakfast but Maria would not eat it. She lay with the duvet over her head and told Lisa to go away. Lisa left the breakfast on her bedside table.

"Eat something, darling, it will help you to feel better." She closed the door behind her but in so doing focused on Maria's form under the duvet and sighed.

Magdalene rang Henry.

"Hello, Henry? Yes, Magdalene here. Sorry but I've got awful news, Maria was taken ill in the night. No, no, not gone to hospital but a high temperature and she's shivering and being sick," she lied.

There was a pregnant pause at Henry's end of the line. He had been up early to pack his bag, shaved, showered and dressed in new chinos and a blue checked shirt. He had tied his burgundy cravat around his neck with self-assurance. "Soon," he had said to himself. "Soon."

He went pale. "What, what are you telling me Magdalene? Not possible, surely she was fine when I left her yesterday!"

"Well, the twins have had some virus that's going around the school and it seems that Maria has picked it up. I'm sorry, Henry but I cannot let her go to Prague." She put the phone down and turned to Lisa who had been watching her and burst into tears.

Under his breath, Henry cursed the twins and those 'bloody lezzers' for allowing this to happen. *Christ,* he thought, *there was nothing wrong with the child yesterday.* He stormed out of the house and into the car as he was determined to check Maria out himself.

Chapter 15

Henry had returned home in a furious rage, disturbing Wendy who was surprised to see him as she had expected him to be in Prague. He swore, cursed and blasphemed about the dykes who wouldn't even let him see Maria.

Wendy had some empathy with his wrath, knowing how much the Prague visit meant to him.

On a weekly basis, Wendy popped in to meet with Mr Horwood to agree the content of the next week's school assembly. His kindly face greeted her and she sat on the other side of his desk as she brought up the subject of Maria.

"She has an amazing talent you know, Mr Horwood," she said, to which Mr Horwood nodded as he rather felt she was stating the obvious. He thought the vicar was a little over the top in her boastfulness about how it was she who discovered Maria but listened, grateful for a break from the pile of routine administration that was overtaking him.

Mrs Elliot came in with steaming mugs of tea printed with the school name, 'St Michael's C. of E.' and a plate of biscuits.

"Oh, Mr Horwood, hearing you both talk about Maria Amari, I have not yet received the birth certificate from her mother. She has completed the school entry form but as you know County is inspecting us next week to ensure all our documentation is in order. Something to do with future numbers and immigration, I think. Shall I write another letter?

I have chased her, you know, and she will have had time by now to order a copy."

"Yes please, Veronica," he replied. He sighed and shot a glance at Wendy. "Better have everything in order. It won't be the teaching that kills me but the bureaucracy in the end. Is there anyone else outstanding?"

"No, Mr Horwood, just Maria."

Mrs Elliot left the room and Wendy registered the conversation deep in her memory. She continued her friendly babble with Mr Horwood and could not wait to get home and tell Henry.

"It doesn't seem much of a coincidence, Henry, that no birth certificate has been produced and the women pull out of Prague at such short notice."

Henry's eyes widened.

"But what could that mean, Wendy? Why hasn't Maria got a birth certificate? Things can easily be lost you know."

"I don't know, Henry, but I believe you that Maria wasn't ill. I've had my suspicions about those two women. Yes, what could it mean? Perhaps she is adopted? Or, perhaps they paid someone else to give birth to her, you know I mean, in their situation, perhaps neither of them wanted to sleep with a man?"

"Well, she's very like her mother, Wendy."

"Same colouring I agree, but her gift does not come from Magdalene."

"Her father, maybe?" said Henry.

"Possibly, dear, what if Maria is not theirs at all?"

"But how could that be?"

"Who knows? But I think that I am going to do a sneaky bit of investigation. Henry, you deserve this chance with Maria and I am going to do my best to make sure it happens for you. I'll make some enquiries."

Henry stared at his sister. For all her resolve to worship her God there was a mean side to her which had never sat well with him. Her revengeful attitude was in conflict with her beliefs but he knew that she would get to the bottom of it and unearth whatever secrets those women were keeping about his protégé, Maria Amari.

It was never clear to Magdalene and Lisa how the authorities found out about them although they did suspect that Henry had something to do with it. Henry had called at the house but they would not let him see Maria, stating that she was in bed asleep and that it was best to leave her, as she had had a fretful night.

A few weeks after the competition date, on a dim and hollow evening, the doorbell rang.

Lisa opened the door to be greeted by a male and female police officer and a female social worker.

"We are here to make enquiries about the parentage and possible abduction of Maria Amari, as we have received information to say that the child is not yours."

"Magdalene's," Lisa said quietly. "You mean Magdalene's child. Come in."

Lisa's manner was fateful as she led the police officers into the cottage. Magdalene looked up from her supper, gasping at the uniformed shapes before her and gave out an anguished cry. Her terrified eyes sought out Lisa's face, which was spectral. She guessed immediately why their visitors were here.

Neither woman bothered to pretend anything but the truth, knowing that each would be found out in the end. A clawing chill filled the room as Magdalene and Lisa were taken away for questioning. They held hands in the back of the police car. Lisa was sobbing but Magdalene sat, brittle with consuming fear and dread. She looked over at Lisa and stroked her hair.

"It'll be all right, darling. It will be all right."

The women knew that it would not be all right, but Magdalene was only trying to comfort Lisa, whose sobs had become uncontrollable.

"What will become of our Maria?" Lisa blurted.

"She'll be fine darling, hush. She's a strong and determined girl. We'll see her again one day Lisa, I know we will. And, if we are separated, remember the 'Ladies of Llangollen.' All of us will be together again one day, you'll see."

Lisa smiled weakly and threw herself across Magdalene, traumatised by the thought of not seeing the two people that meant the most to her in the world. Magdalene continued to stroke her hair in a maternal fashion until they reached the police station.

Maria liked the social worker lady. She had hair the colour of beer and lines creased her nose. She was trim and wore jeans with a blouse and blue cardigan tied at the waist by a belt with a large buckle. Her sneakers were bright red. She had brought Maria some juice in the artificially lit room where they sat on pale green plastic chairs. There were rough blue carpet tiles under her feet. Angie, for this was the social worker's name, encouraged Maria to sit on the floor next to her and together they built a house out of odd bits of building blocks. Maria liked her smell and liked the colour of her skin. Angie was dual heritage. She had a black father and a white mother. Maria thought that she must have picked all the best bits from her parent's faces as she was very nice-looking. When she smiled there was a large gap in her teeth, which held some fascination for Maria.

At that moment, the male policeman that she had met at the house came in.

"Angie, there's no DNA match. This is an abduction and we are just about to charge the two women. All right?"

Angie looked at the little girl, and Maria noticed the change in her expression.

"Why are you sad?"

"I'm not sad, Maria, but there are lots of things we are going to have to talk about. It will be fun. Not tonight though, as you are having a special treat. You are coming to stay at my house. Would you like that?"

"Yes, I would. And Mo, Mo can come too, can't he?"

"Is he here right now?"

"No, but he will be tomorrow," Maria replied.

"Then I can't wait to meet him."

Maria woke in a navy blue painted box room and blinked. *Where was she?* Then she remembered. There was a tap on the door and Angie came in and took her down for breakfast.

It took all the services a month to discover Maria's natural birth mother. The press had got hold of the story and it was splashed all over the tabloids. Front page headlines: 'Genius Girl Snatched – Who Is Her Mother?'

There was an appeal on a television 'Crimewatch' programme asking anyone for any information about Maria. There were pictures of her everywhere.

This was how Magdalene and Lisa gleaned that Maria was named 'Sapphire Emerald Mortimer' and she was in fact now seven years old. Her birth date was 13th March. *A Pisces*, thought Lisa in her prison cell. It was an odd thing to come to her mind in such circumstances but it helped her to understand Maria's musical ability. Pisceans were normally musical, *like George Harrison,* she thought, who bore no comparison to Maria but his name popped inexplicably into her head and she wondered what Maria was doing now. Where was she?

Emily Mortimer had come forward after seeing the headline picture of Maria at a news stand on her way to buy her drugs. She sniffed loudly and went closer to look at the picture. She saw her own eyes staring back out at her.

When questioned by the police why she had never reported Maria as missing, she had replied that she didn't think they would believe her.

The DNA matches confirmed Emily as the birth mother and Angie and her team worked quickly to reunite the lost child with her new-found parent.

Emily received substantial amounts of cash for her story. She was portrayed as the poor woman who had her child stolen by a pair of lesbians just because she had social problems and had been discarded by her parents, the tabloids said. Her drug addiction was no fault of her own, more because of her circumstances, abandoned by her wealthy parents, they said. One of the daily newspapers sponsored her to 'convalesce' in the 'Priory' for six months; 'Abducted Child's Mother Getting Clean' it reported, and when she came out she was indeed clean.

With some of the cash from the newspapers and magazines she tidied up her flat and bought second-hand items of furniture. In the nine months since she had claimed Maria she was ready to have her back.

Angie was worried. She had placed Maria with a loving foster family in Highgate. Admittedly the whole family were a bit eccentric, but very musical. She hoped that Maria would find some solace. She telephoned Jenny regularly for updates and Jenny told her that Maria was definitely missing the lesbians but seemed more concerned about someone called Mo, Mo?

Angie informed her that Mo, Mo was Maria's imaginary friend and suggested that maybe Jenny should include Mo, Mo in any games that her two sons would play with Maria. Jenny and the boys tried but Maria was withdrawn. She said they were all stupid because Mo, Mo was at Rose Cottage and she wanted to go back and see him.

"She's quite remote and she hasn't been near the piano, I'm afraid. She is eating and I actually think she has grown a bit. Edgar and Jonty find her a strange little creature, but they are both patient with her in their own way. Will she really have to go back to her mother?"

Angie replied, "Yes." Jenny sighed and Angie understood the meaning of the sigh, as she was worried too.

When Angie arrived with Maria at the tower block the press were already waiting. She pushed her way through, trying to protect Maria as she headed for the stairs, up two flights to the first floor.

Emily was standing at the doorway as a television hair artist swept her thin strands of hair into a high pony tail, which gave her a teenage look. Emily wore a long-sleeved black lace dress to cover her tattoos and needle holes. She looked attractive, and the dress showed off her petite frame. The television crew were huddled together, anticipating the moment when mother and child would first meet in this national sensational story.

Maria was sullen. She held her head low not wanting to meet any grown-ups eye to eye. She was tired and didn't want to leave Angie.

Bending down on one knee with outstretched arms, Emily called Sapphire into her arms and Maria felt a push in her back from one of the television crew, forcing her to move closer to this woman who Angie had said was her real mother.

Of course, Angie had previously set-up many more discrete meetings between Emily and Maria in the community room at her offices but this was like a circus, a pandemonium of obsession.

Emily wrapped her arms around 'her Sapphire' and led her into the space behind the filthy door and melee of press reporters.

Once inside Angie did the preliminary form filling and inspected the bare flat. Emily had painted Maria's room lilac and had bought a single bed and a chest of drawers. The room wasn't big enough for a wardrobe. There was a cheap nylon red carpet and frilly thin pink curtains at the window which looked out over the front of the building.

Maria felt indifferent about Emily. She missed her other mummy and Lisa and Henry and the piano. Emily showed Maria her bedroom and gave her a can of fizzy drink and a packet of crisps.

"I'll come and visit you next week, Maria," Angie said.

"Her name is Sapphire now, if you don't mind," retorted Emily.

Angie ignored her and smiled down at Maria.

"Next week, Maria." Maria smiled mournfully back at her and walked into her new bedroom.

Angie left, charging through the press and TV hullaballoo on the landing. She drove away in her car with an uneasy feeling.

Emily went into the bedroom and sat on the bed where Maria was sitting, gazing at what seemed nothing. Emily had cut out some Disney characters and pasted them on to her lilac walls.

She put her arm around Maria.

"I know this is very strange for you darling, but I'm your mummy now. I'm your real mummy, not like those witches who stole you away."

"They're not witches," said Maria. "Go away, I hate you!"

Emily got up to leave.

"Darling, it will take time for us to get to know one another but you will have to get used to it. I'll make you some beans on toast for tea," she said, as if this was the answer to all Maria's woes.

Maria tried to doze, hearing the TV, which was at full volume. She got out of bed and crept to the door, opening it slightly. Her mother was sprawled on the couch watching a talent show and she noticed Maria out of the corner of her eye.

"I thought you would come out when you was hungry. I made you some beans on toast ages ago but you was fast asleep. I'll heat the plate in the microwave."

Maria sat on the chair and watched her mother put the plate into the steel box and pour some milk into a plastic beaker. When the microwave pinged she brought her the food and drink on a tray and Maria sat in silence, eating her supper watching the television. No words parted between them.

This was the pattern for a few days until a visitor came. He was a man. Maria could not work out how old he was, as his face was covered in spots and scars, and his blue jeans were tatty and dirty. He wore a brown leather jacket and a pale green washed-out shirt.

"Aw, fank God you've come," said Emily. "I am going out of my head with boredom sat in 'ere every day watching over her." They both looked over at Maria, who was still in her flimsy pyjamas. Her hair had not been brushed because she had screamed when Emily had tried to manage the tangles, so Emily didn't bother to carry on. She had shown Maria where there was a flannel and towel in the bathroom and a pink toothbrush of her own.

"'spect yer old enouf to do all that yourself by now?"

Maria stared at the woman who called herself her mother. This woman, for whom she felt nothing. She did not understand why Magdalene and Lisa had forsaken her. She missed them so much that it hurt her tummy.

Emily's mood had changed radically in only a few days and she had barely managed to cook Maria any more meals, instead showing her how to use the toaster. There were some digestive biscuits in a torn packet where the contents were crumbled and spilling out. Maria helped herself to those as the visitor and Emily watched her.

"You gonna bring back a fix, right?" the visitor asked.

"Yeah apparently Dave's got some good stuff. Bleeding priceless by all accounts. Just watch her until I come back. Put the telly on, she likes that."

Emily reverted to this accent when she was in the presence of people like her present company. There was still a spark of shame inside her. She never wanted people to know that she had come from a very middle-class family. Both her parents were doctors but they had washed their hands of her some time ago. Giving up the crusade of trying to bring their daughter home and off drugs was beyond them. They had tried everything in their doctor books and everything not in their doctor books. Each gave up the ghost of their daughter to the world she had created for herself. Her parents lived with the despair and the never-knowing like an unspoken curse that hung on a chain around their necks, dreading the day when the phone would ring with bad news about their only child.

Emily didn't know where that shame came from, particularly as she had prostituted herself to earn money to pay for her drug addiction. That's when Maria had come along quite unexpectedly. It was amazing that Maria had survived the birth; she was a tiny mite when she was born and already hooked on the drugs her mother was feeding her in the womb. No-one seemed to care about her or her baby and now she didn't care anymore, either.

The visitor could see her agitation as he nodded and picked up the remote. He found a football match and watched intently, occasionally swearing at the television.

Maria sloped off to her room. She didn't know what time it was as there were no clocks in the house and she had left her Cinderella watch at home. The December sky was drawing in with dark dank tousles of slate, streaked dimly with nickel clouds. She watched as first flurries of snow pattered at her window. Maria looked out at the madding crowd of London. There was a muffled noise of cars and trains and she saw hazy lights and a red London bus. In the distance she saw the warm light of a house and the aura from it reminded her of home.

At this point she heard the front door bang and she thought it was Emily returning. There was no noise apart from the blaring of the TV. She was hungry and went out to make some toast the way that Emily had shown her. She looked at the vacant chair where the visitor had sat and was now gone. She realised she was alone.

Going back to her bedroom, Maria dressed and packed a few small things in her rucksack. She looked out of the window but could only see a blanket of white as the snow grew thick and sheer against it.

She went to the front door but it was locked. *It must have locked when that man banged it,* she thought. Maria began to cry, the tears tumbling down her cheeks. She was cold and hungry and she wanted Mo, Mo.

After a while she got up to go back to her room. She pulled the chest of drawers as far as she could beneath the window. Its frame was made of metal and was black with condensation and dirt. As Maria pulled at the thin curtain she noticed a latch. She tugged it and the window slid across easily. As the window slid open a burst of cold air caught the back of her throat and she blinked and coughed. The draft was icy and drove into her bones.

She took off her coat and put on another jumper, and then pulled the coat back on over that. As she looked down she saw a mound like a hill. It looked soft and the snowflakes pittered and pattered over the top. She imagined that it was a giant's chair, a place where he may come to rest.

Steadily, she climbed on to the ledge of the window where she sat, her little bottom teetering on its edge, and she kicked her wellies against the wall. The city looked like magic as the hues of the snow picked out the urban starlight. Maria looked up to the sky where the snow was relentless.

Then she fell.

Chapter 16

Michael and Steven had hired a white van to remove their mother's things from the flat across the hall from Emily. Their mother had moved out about a month ago but she still hadn't got around to clearing out odds bits of furniture and utility items.

Both men were relieved that they had finally persuaded their mother to move. She had received a constant barrage of press and media at her door, asking her questions about Emily. She had decided not to answer the door and both Michael and Steven had to ring her three times beforehand from their mobiles as a code so that she knew it was them waiting to be let in.

Queenie had made up her own mind about moving. She had resisted for quite a while but her boys were right, it was not a nice place to live any more and they were doing so well with their wives, families and occupations that she thought it would be nicer to be closer to them. There was a new build of homes near to the old Arsenal ground and the boys had taken on a mortgage between them to provide her with a small one-bedroom flat. The flat was fresh and clean and still smelled of paint. In her new building were lots of single people and it wasn't long before she made new friends and she began to think why she had not chosen to move before. '*Silly stubborn woman*' is what her dead husband would have said, she thought. She was glad to move away and when all the fuss and publicity arose over that little girl, she was more than pleased to go.

Michael had jumped out of the passenger side of the van and pulled the door across to shut. He habitually took his phone out of his pocket to check if he had any calls and he caught sight of something falling out of the corner of his eye. He wasn't sure at first but heard a sickening thud. He looked to where the sound came from just as his brother joined him from the other side of the van.

"You all right, Mike?"

"Something just fell out of that window up there, look, the one with the curtains flapping outside of it."

Steven looked up at where Michael was pointing.

"Probably someone throwing out rubbish," he said but Michael was unsure.

He walked over to the skip and looked over the top. The virginal snow was corrupted by the single flow of red liquid oozing and tracing its way from a little girl's head through the landscape created by the rubbish below.

"Oh my God! Steven, call an ambulance QUICK! It's a child!"

Chapter 17

Mr McPhearson was Scottish. He was of the old school, a straight back and a no-nonsense sort of a chap. His hair was white now but the hairs that grew from his nose and his ears hinted at his previous Celtic red hair. When he was young he never drank alcohol as he wanted to keep his hands steady. These days he always had a wee whisky before bedtime to keep his hands from trembling. His cheeks gave away his secret habit as they were blushed in purple.

All the nurses called him 'Mr Mc-Fear-Some', as they did fear him. Certainly the student nurses found him scary but the old hands knew him better and admired his skill and tenacity as a doctor.

Maria had been in his care from the very beginning. He had induced her coma at first so that her brain had time to heal and shrink back to its normal size. She was a tiny bundle, he remembered, pale and deathly. She had two broken legs and from this he summarised that she must have landed on them. It was unfortunate that she had caught her head on the rim of the skip; she might otherwise be awake now and at school and suffering teenage angst like normal girls her age.

That was, as he checked the chart clipped at the end of her bed where he kept the year scribed at the top to remind him, seven years ago.

Her legs had mended and grown. Her hair had grown too. The nurses asked Mr McPhearson if they could cut it as it was easier to maintain but he always refused, as for him it was a sign that this child was still alive and all other functions were stabilised. The nurses had plaited it into a long braid down her back.

He sat by her bed and held her hand. She was in a private room, away from prying eyes. The medical paraphernalia she was hooked to kept a measure of all Maria's statistics. Looking at these machines he knew the rate of her heartbeat, the pulsating of her blood coursing through her body, her temperature, the activity of her lungs, but he knew he would never know her dreams. The good news was that she was dreaming and she had rapid eye movement on numerous occasions.

"Before I die would be nice," he said in an ironic jokey sort of way as he stroked his thumb on her palm.

"Wake up, Maria."

Maria did not respond, and he hadn't really expected her to. He had ordered the nurses to bring in compact discs of the latest trends in boy bands and they obliged by turning the volume up high until he said he could not stand it any longer and asked for it to be altered to a low murmur.

He had ordered that the TV be switched on. Then he ordered it to be switched off and then he ordered for it to be switched back on again. He wanted to stimulate Maria into waking but the normal channels weren't working.

Recently, one of the women who had abducted the child had written to him from prison. . He read her letter with interest and was surprised to learn that a cell mate had smuggled it to him upon her release. She had left broad handwriting on the envelope at reception saying, 'This letter is only for the eyes of the doctor caring for Maria Amari.'

In her letter, Lisa informed him that one way to wake Maria would be to play Mozart to her. She loved him, she said in her letter and described Maria's imaginary friend called 'Mo, Mo' the greatest composer who ever lived. She had a strong bond with her imaginary friend, and although she may

113

be too old now for such childish things, it may well be worth trying.

Lisa and Magdalene, coincidentally, had been sentenced on that fateful day when Maria tumbled through the snow flying towards the council skip. The Judge was fairly lenient with the couple as there was no doubt that they only wanted to care for her, but they had broken the law and he gave them each thirteen years imprisonment. Lisa and Magdalene were sent to two different institutions to serve out their 'time.'

Magdalene clearly understood the consequences of her actions. She blamed herself. It was she who had seen Maria that day through the crack of the door. She was less worried about herself as she was coping with prison life, but fretted constantly about Lisa. The last time she had seen her was in Court and she had looked pale and frail. She wondered how Lisa had reacted to the devastating news about Maria's fall. The two lovers were at least allowed to write to one another and Magdalene's letters were positive and forward-thinking in her determination that the three would be together once more and that Maria would wake up.

Lisa's thoughts were more about getting through each day. She was tortured by the thought of Maria in a coma and longed to be by her bedside to touch her fingers. She made peace with herself about Mo, Mo and wished and prayed for him to visit Maria in her dreams so that she would wake. Deep inside, each woman knew that she would, one day.

Mr McPhearson smiled at Maria. He wondered what she would think, when or if she ever woke. Her own mother was now dead from a drug overdose - by a same twist of fate she died on the day of Maria's fall. Emily had gone to meet her dealer armed with her story pay-off cash and was too desperate and greedy to wait until she got back to her flat so she loaded up under a bridge that crossed over a canal. She was found dead and slumped against the wall, the needle still in her hand. The Post Mortem showed a high quality drug substance, and because her body was not used to the intake of a good grade drug it had killed her.

His thoughts drifted as he looked out over the skyline. The cobalt sky was cloudless and the rays of the sun beat down across the Thames where the Houses of Parliament bathed in its blonde light. It was one of the hottest summers on record and he was looking forward to his round of golf at the weekend.

Angie the Social Worker arrived and interrupted his thoughts. He let go of Maria's hand and smiled up at her. He shook his head before Angie could ask the obvious question about Maria's awakening and moved out of the chair so that Angie could sit down.

She took Maria's hand into her own and stroked it gently.

"Come on Maria," she said.

The machines bleeped and the lines on her brain activity chart moved randomly up and down. Maria's eyes were moving rapidly and Angie thought that Maria must be dreaming again, and wondered what visions would keep a little girl asleep for seven years?

Mr McPhearson left the room with "see you next week?"

Angie nodded. His words brought back a memory of when she had left Maria behind in the dingy flat with her mother. She had promised to come back. As it turned out, in fact she had, every Wednesday afternoon for seven years. The hospital staff knew her on first name terms and brought her mugs of tea if they weren't too busy with other patients on the ward.

She and Mr McPhearson had done what Lisa had asked and played Mozart after Mozart but nothing moved Maria into waking up.

The hospital was always unbearably hot, the air was stale as no window could be opened and Angie, seeing that all the staff were busy, went out to get some water. When she came back into the room she stared, rooted to the spot as Maria seemed to be trying to open her eyes. She dropped the water and shouted to the nurses at the reception desk,

"Quick, quick, page Mr McPhearson, I think Maria is waking up!"

Everything was fuzzy and Maria could only make out shapes. The room was filled with light and it hurt her eyes. In the distance she could hear people talking and moving around her, dressed in white like angels. She thought that she must be dead and in heaven and she fixed her eyes more keenly to see if she could pick out Mozart from the shuffling crowd around her.

One of the angels put his hand on her head and said, "Maria, can you hear me? I'm Mr McPhearson and you are in hospital. You had a nasty fall but you are OK now. Maria? Maria?"

Maria looked up at him and said, "Hospital?"

A conjoined sigh of relief combed the room, searching for an exit, but lingered there like an eagle soaring on thermals.

Over the next few weeks it was a relief to Angie to see the machines gradually being removed and the tubes coming out of Maria's body. Her outline under the stark white hospital sheets was long and she had indeed grown. The nurses had brought her some pyjamas and helped Maria to the shower so she looked fresh and clean with her dark long locks plaited neatly, nestling into the curve of her swan-like neck.

Banners and balloons decorated the room and a cake lay on the side table half eaten. Angie thought it was a good cause to celebrate; the nurses had obviously brought them in. She was grinning as she sat in the chair and placed Maria's hand into her own.

"How are you feeling? Any pain?"

Maria shook her head.

"I'm just confused about everything, Angie." Maria began to cry.

Angie jumped up and put her arms around her.

"It will take time Maria, you have been asleep for seven years and there are some big adjustments that you are going to have to make. You are a teenager now and you will need to adjust to that. The psychologists will spend a lot of time working with you to help you feel better. Come on, luv."

Angie tightened her grip around Maria who had blossomed in her sleep into a beautiful young woman. Maria made Angie think of a butterfly locked in its chrysalis only to open and flutter to chase sunbeams. It was a good analogy, she thought.

The psychologists worked wonders with Maria. They introduced a specialised children's' counsellor and within six months of waking up she was ready to leave her hospital bed.

Angie had made Maria her priority. She had struggled through the inevitable case report that delved critically into the multi-service care of Maria. In her own heart she felt she had done nothing wrong and had followed the protocol to the last degree. Maria's case was splashed all over the newspapers and the 'scandal' fed the papers and magazines with another good twelve month revival of news following the death of Emily and the court case against Lisa and Magdalene.

Angie was cleared of any wrongdoing, which was of some relief to her as she needed her job to support her growing family. Things hadn't worked out so well with Vince in the end and she found herself a single parent. Stuart was at university now and Tabatha was just finishing A' levels. They had only been a bit older than Maria on the day that she fell, she thought, and now her son towered over her and her daughter was proving to be as academic as her brother. Vince did help out financially and saw the children regularly. Angie felt that she was nearing the end of a long period of childcare filled with trials, tantrums and tribulations. Tabatha would be off in the autumn and now it was time for Angie to have some 'me' time.

I should tell them, she suddenly thought. *Magdalene and Lisa. I'll write.*

Lisa and Magdalene received the letters from Angie and wept for joy. Magdalene began to hatch her plan to track down Maria's whereabouts and those thoughts of gladness kept the lovers alive with vigour until the end of their sentences, which were being shortened for good behaviour.

Angie had been in touch with Jenny and her husband Seb in Highgate and they had agreed to take Maria back. Their boys had grown too during the time Maria was dreaming. Edgar was nineteen and at Bristol reading English and Jonty was seventeen, just finishing his first year of A' levels. Jonty wanted to be a forensic scientist and when he was not at school or playing sports he would sit on the bed in his room watching recorded episodes of murder and crime series.

Jenny and Seb were rather Bohemian in their outlook. Jenny wore floaty skirts and dresses and tied lavish silk scarves around her messy hair. She even smoked coloured cigarettes from a long cigarette holder, which wasn't often but was rather dramatic. Jenny wrote for a weekly arts magazine and was as scatty as a scarecrow. It showed in her home, which was untidy. Bookshelves lined walls in every room, including the loos, gathering dust and woodworm. Her cleaner had stopped trying to clean beneath anything that was fixed down, instead skirting around objects and books and magazines and sport bags filled with unwashed sports gear and Jonty's bicycle that lived in the hallway.

The house was a traditional four-floor terrace with a thin garden that ran symmetrically with its neighbours on either side. You could not see the bottom of the garden as it was obscured by lilac trees, overgrown rhododendrons and azaleas. A worn broken musical chime hung listlessly and there were holes in the ground where perhaps weasels or stoats had burrowed through.

In this mayhem Seb closed his eyes and inhaled on his spliff. "Peace, peace..."

He tapped the keys on the piano as the smoke from his spliff whiffed up from his nostrils, licking his forehead and settling in wisps in his chestnut hair which fell haphazardly over his face.

Seb wrote music for big advertising companies. He had been married to Jenny for nearly twenty five years, yet he had changed little from his wedding day photos. He was having an affair with a girl working at one of his major clients and they met, on occasion, at a smart hotel where they had sex until they had to return home to their perspective partners. She knew the score, he was never going to marry her and it was just a bit of fun, he thought. He was pretty certain the affair would fizzle out as she was already becoming boring to him, chatting as she did, as he lay naked on his back studying the ceiling after each of them had screamed their orgasms to one another. Fiona laboured on a bit about how much she yearned for a baby.

"Do you think my figure will go?" she had asked him one sunny afternoon as they lay together.

"You know, if I have a baby?"

Seb sat up and looked at her bare and inviting flat stomach stretched out towards her pink nipples, pert on her chest.

"Fiona darling," he said. "Look, just get on and have a baby but make sure it's not mine!"

Fiona looked upset.

"Now come on, don't be silly. I'll be surprised if you can grow a baby in that tiny belly of yours." He heaved himself on top of her, having sex with her for what he knew would be the last time.

He suspected that Jenny was having a fling too, with one of the book club guys, but such was their relationship that neither minded nor cared to enquire about the other. It would only rock the boat, and things were fine just as they were, it seemed to him.

He learned about Maria coming back to stay with some reluctance. Jenny was standing in the kitchen, which was a tip and smelled a bit like rotten cabbage.

"All right Jen," he said. "But I'm not getting involved, you are going to have to deal with any issues." His wife was wearing a silk kimono over a black all-in-one cat suit. She had a good figure for her age and he never minded making love to Jenny when he got the chance. She was smoking a purple cigarette from her holder, blowing the smoke into the air with her chin uplifted. *God,* he thought. *She thinks she's bloody Zsa Zsa Gabor*, and left the room with a large glass of wine that she had poured for him.

Jenny visited Maria in hospital and under the guidance of the experts she agreed to take Maria home. Angie realised the couple were slightly off the conventional mark but she sensed that the Goldstein's would be a good environment for Maria to fit into.

Maria kissed the staff goodbye and Mr McPhearson was noted to have a tear or two as he waved Maria off. He denied it, of course, when the nursing staff teased him later.

Jenny led her out of the hospital and over Westminster Bridge to the taxi bays. She was worried and thought she should have brought the car, but Maria sat quietly taking in the views on the journey back to Highgate. Jenny smiled at her, not knowing what to say.

"I've made up the spare room for you Maria. It's where you slept before. Do you remember?"

Maria remembered and nodded. She wasn't in the mood for talking. She was thinking about how she was going to bring Mo, Mo back into her life. *He will come,* she thought. *I know he will come, for I dreamed about him there.*

Chapter 18

Life wasn't as chaotic as it seemed at the Goldstein's, it just seemed that way because nothing was ever planned or organised or put away. The men left in the house seemed to accept the mess and Jenny was certainly not the type to perform housework. She was rarely at home and was either out at lunch dates with her agent or visiting friends or art galleries, or visiting the book club group.

The Goldsteins had the good grace to leave Maria on her own for a while to get used to her new surroundings. She was delighted one day when a marmalade cat came to her room and leapt onto her bed beside her, purring away contentedly. She stroked his soft fur and examined the collar to discover the cat wasn't a he but a she, and was called Trixie. It had the family phone number on a tag should it ever be lost and found. Trixie would sometimes sit on the windowsill, bathing in the sunshine that leaked through the sash window and Maria liked to see her sat there like a queen.

Maria was now fourteen and thoughts were turning to the new school term. Jenny thought it would be lovely for Maria to walk to school with Jonty, who protested too much at the idea. Jenny took in Maria's form as she languidly lay on the couch. She had thrown off the magazines to make room and Trixie was curled next to her, enjoying the soft strokes from Maria's sculptured hand. *She is a stunning looking girl, I'm sure Jonty won't mind the least bit,* Jenny thought.

Maria settled down well in the new environment. She had quickly come to terms with her lost seven years and was excited about being a teenager. Her period started and Jenny fussed and said that they should all throw a party to celebrate Maria's womanhood. Jonty looked disgusted at the idea and Seb rolled his eyes.

"Leave the poor girl alone," he said.

Maria felt proud that she was now a woman but declined Jenny's idea, politely suggesting instead that perhaps the two of them could go out for a meal? She was really beginning to like Jenny. *Yes, she is a bit eccentric,* she thought as she looked around the room at Jonty and Seb talking about the football scores, at Jenny leaned against the kitchen top, yet she felt at home. Soon, she felt sure, it would be Mo, Mo's home too.

Jenny and Seb almost missed waving Maria off to her new school as they had both overslept having spent the evening drinking and dining with friends.

Maria had been up at 6 o'clock and showered and dressed in her new uniform. It comprised of a blue and green plaid skirt, blue blouse, grey socks with a blue trim and a blue jumper with a green trim. Her shoes were new and polished. She brushed her hair and braided two familiar plaits. Her hair reached past her bottom and the ends were lighter than the rest.

She shook out some cereal and milk into a bowl and filled the kettle. She made tea and took up a mug to Jonty who had disappeared under his duvet as she opened the curtains.

"Oh, the light, the light! You are cruel, Maria."

He walked close to her side on the way to school and friends and groups of friends gathered as they went along. "This is Maria," Jonty repeatedly phrased and his mates cheekily smirked at Jonty, wondering where he had got this vision that was now walking beside him.

Jonty went off to the VI Form Block and directed Maria to her classroom. There was a group of girls huddled together, their chatter filled the room loudly and stopped as Maria entered the room.

Naturally inquisitive, the coterie took in her beauty, stunned momentarily into quiet. Then one girl came up and said,

"Hello, I'm Annabella."

From that day Maria and Annabella became firm friends and as it turned out Annabella lived on the street parallel to Maria's, and the parents all knew each other.

Maria and Annabella had 'sleepovers' and rarely parted company.

Maria had vivid dreams and sometimes would wake Annabella, talking aloud. She spoke to Jenny about it, who reassured her. Maria had taken a heck of a crack on the head, she told her, and had been asleep for seven years, so she was entitled to dream, which placated Annabella somewhat.

Shortly after the Christmas holidays commenced, Christmas not being an event the Goldsteins celebrated, Jonty needed to pee in the middle of the night, his bladder full with beer he had drunk with his father watching a football match on TV. He had to pass Maria's room, the door was ajar and he heard her talking. It was late but he thought it was probably Annabella. On the way back he stopped. Maria was speaking in German, clearly having a conversation with someone he couldn't see. He shrugged his shoulders, assuming it was Annabella whom he was sure had a crush on him. He looked at himself in the large mirror and rubbed his hands through his hair and with a vain purse of the lips, blew himself a kiss and went back to bed.

Jonty forgot all about it until a month or so later when the same thing happened again. The holidays were over and it was his last term at school. If he did well in his exams, dad had promised him a car and driving lessons. His parents had done the same for Edgar and he was eager to have his own wheels.

This time he had been 'out on the lash' with his mates and had come home drunk, staggering up to his room where he flopped on the bed fully clothed and fell asleep. He woke with a dry mouth and a full bladder.

Passing Maria's room, he heard her talking in German.

"Ich werde Mo, Mo. Ich simme die Zeit reif ist für mich und ich werde fragen, Seb." (I will Mo, Mo. I agree the time is right for me and I will ask Seb tomorrow if I can play on his piano).

"Miene Liebe, meine Venus tun das für mich mein Schatz Maria." (My love, my Venus, do this for me my darling Maria)?

Jonty thought he heard a male voice, and opened the door a little further so he could see who Maria was talking to. She was sat on the bed with her arms placed as if she was holding someone, but there was no one there that he could see. *Bloody odd girl,* he thought, and went back to bed.

Synagogue visits were on a Friday after school and Jenny told Maria that she didn't have to attend because she wasn't Jewish. Annabella was usually at the Synagogue too, so Maria would let herself in and go to her room to read magazines or books, or listen to a current popular CD. Often, during these times Maria would call Mozart to come to her. He would appear sitting on her bed, stroking her hair and talking about his music. Maria would listen to his words intently, making notes in her head so that she could understand the emotion behind his compositions. He would kiss her gently on the cheeks and hold her hands.

Saturday morning came along, shoved upon the nation briskly by the bustle of milk and newspaper deliveries. Saturdays were slothful at the Goldstein's. At a leisurely breakfast in the kitchen - which was looking tidier since Maria had lived there, as she enjoyed cleaning it up - Maria asked Seb if she could play his piano.

Seb put the paper on the table and looked atop his reading glasses at Jenny, who was trying to signal to him that this was going to be a profound moment for Maria.

Seb ignored Jenny and reached out to hold Maria's hand.

"I would be delighted, Maria," he said. Whenever you want, just help yourself, no need to ask."

"Thank you," Maria said, and noticed that Jenny was fidgeting.

"That reminds me," said Jonty. "Maria was speaking German to some invisible lover in her sleep last night. I saw you in your room Maria, jabbering away, 'Miene Liebe, meine Venus'.

"Nonsense," said Jenny. "Maria can't speak German."

"Yes she fuckin' well can!"

"Jonty, don't say fuckin' in front of your mother and Maria."

"Dad, you just said fuckin'."

"That's different," his father replied.

Maria stood up and looked Jonty straight in the eye.

"Don't ever fuckin' well spy on me again!" she said and left the room in a rage.

Jonty looked over at his father. "Are you gonna tell her not to say fuckin'?"

Jenny reprimanded him and told him not to tease Maria.

"Poor girl only wanted to play the piano," she said. Seb picked up his paper and sipped his coffee.

"Just hope we haven't all put her off playing again," he said from behind the paper.

After she had flung things into the dishwasher, Jenny went upstairs to speak with Maria. She tapped on the door gently and found Maria sprawled across the bed with one of her long legs over the edge, touching the floor.

"Maria luv, can I talk to you?" Maria made a teenage grunting sound that Jenny recognised to mean yes. She sat on the bed and Maria sat up with her back against the headboard. Her eyes were red from where she had been crying. Jenny tucked a loose strand of her hair behind her ear and caressed her face.

"Maria, you had a nasty bump on the head, and all those years in that coma, who knows what may have happened to your brain? It is quite possible something somewhere has triggered a memory from the past and you learned German without realising it. When you were sleeping Mr McPhearson insisted on playing you all sorts of sounds to wake you up. Maybe he played a German language tape. Who knows?" Her voice was soft and quiet. She felt that she and Maria were bonding and she enjoyed having a female around the house. Maria was certainly making an impact as she had never seen the house so tidy and Mrs Potter was making inroads into the years of dust and grime. Maria had even managed to persuade Jonty to keep his bicycle in the garden shed which made the hall seem so much bigger.

"I can speak German, Jenny. It's weird how I know the language, but I can and it's something I share with Mo, Mo."

"Mo, Mo!? Your imaginary friend from when you were a child?"

"He's not imaginary, Jenny. He comes to my room and we are falling in love. I am just upset with Jonty for spying on me."

Jenny surveyed the teenager in front of her. She had to take Maria shopping recently as her boobs were in definite need of a larger sized bra, and without realising it Maria was distracting the men in the house. She was tall for her age, about 5' 6", she thought, and her skin was creamy but it was her eyes, her deep and melodious eyes that were full of mystery that gave Maria an innocent look of promises and secrets.

"Darling, I am not sure I could ever blame any man for falling in love with you. You are gorgeous, and Jonty informs me that you have many admirers at school?"

"I'm not interested in them; I am only interested in Mo, Mo."

"OK. Fair enough, I am not the right person to tell you to be monogamous; it's your choice, darling. Are you going to come down and play the piano?"

"Maybe later."

When Jenny came into the kitchen Jonty had already left to go to Stamford Bridge with some friends. He and his father were avid Chelsea supporters for a reason that Jenny could never work out, as neither of them had been born in Chelsea.

"She OK?" he asked.

"Yes fine. I think she may come down later to play the piano."

"Oh, good. I am looking forward to hearing our little wonder."

Maria went to the bathroom to wash her face and tidy her hair. Her reflection showed her a beautiful face with faint freckles on her nose and long lashes across her almond shaped eyes. Mozart was standing behind her.

"Es ist Zeit Maria?" (It is time, Maria)?

"Yes, it is time."

Chapter 19

Jenny and Seb were sifting through the papers and discussing Jenny's last article in the weekly magazine.

"You are such a hypocrite, darling..," Seb was saying.

Maria opened the door into the room where Seb composed his advertising ditties for radio and TV. This room at least had some order to it. You could actually see carpet and the shelves were stacked uniformly with music books. The fireplace looked like it had never been used and the room smelled of tobacco with a stimulating scent that pricked at Maria's nostrils. The floor was exposed and a Persian rug squared off the seating area made up of a leather two-seater and a reclining chair. A coffee table had sheets of music written in Seb's scrawl weighted down by a squat Buddha.

Maria made her way to the grand piano nestled into the corner as if it had always sat there, looking snug and comfortable. The lid was down and she made her way to sit on the stool. Would she remember? Would she?

Maria tentatively opened the lid. The ebony and ivory startled her. The length of the scales seemed vast. Then she heard Mo, Mo come in and sit next to her.

"I will hold your hands and we will play together."

Seb and Jenny heard her at the same moment. She was playing Mozart's Piano Sonata No.11. They exchanged looks. Seb put down his paper and moved towards his room. The door was open. Jenny followed, not wanting to miss out on anything.

Maria was moderately inclining her head from side to side, her long fingers sparkling across the keys. Jenny's mouth was wide open but Seb simply stood still, and when she finished the last soulful note he put his hands together. Jenny didn't know what to do so followed suit. Maria turned and watched them clapping and felt that thrill from long ago. Mozart leaned in to kiss her and she lifted her shoulders and leant her cheek to one side so she could feel the warmth of his lips on her skin.

"Thank you, miene liebe."

After that day, Maria saw less of Annabella who was beginning to tire her with her teenage meanderings. All Maria wanted to do was practice. Seb was an amazing support, choosing to work in the kitchen on his electric keyboard. He told her that the piano was more deserving of her nimble fingers rather than his. He confessed that it was helping his marriage to Jenny as they actually were conversing in a milder manner, owing to the fact that he was forced to compose in the kitchen where he was less cut off from his wife. She had even shared a spliff with him the other day, he said.

Maria was in the zone. Jonty had stopped walking with her to school as the Easter holidays had gone by and he only needed to go in for exams. Maria felt sure that he would do well; he was clever and taught her loads of stuff for maths that she would otherwise have struggled with. It was obvious to her that this part of her brain had been damaged in her fall, because when she was a child she could have done all those mathematical problems standing on her head.

The summer came and after that Maria moved up a year at school. The boys in her year had given up on pursuing her romantically and called her names. "Here comes the frigid one", they would say and some called her a 'lezzer'. She was still friends with Annabella, although they didn't meet up so much now.

Maria had made her choices for her GCSE's (General Certificate of Education) and the school had made a decision to move her up a year as she was so bright and clever. The school was sure she was capable of passing the ten GCSE's that she had chosen with 'A' stars. Maria had already entered and passed her Grade 8 in piano. She had passed this about eight years ago, but she wanted to prove to herself that she could still do it, and she passed the test easily and was given a special prize on Speech Day for 'Outstanding Musical Newcomer'.

The following summer, when Jonty was at Cardiff University studying Forensic Science, Jenny asked Maria how she was getting on.

"I want to go to the Royal Academy of Music," she informed Jenny. "I think I could get a scholarship."

"Right," said Jenny. "I'll ring them up tomorrow and find out what we have to do."

Each night before she slept, Maria summoned Mozart to her room. Lately he had become tired, for in his dimension he was nearing his early death aged thirty-five. Maria had known him all her life and she began to mourn his death before the day had even come. It was awful for her to see him deteriorate. He no longer whispered sweet nothings in her ear or undressed her casually in order to take her naked in his arms. He no longer made love to her. She had become a trusted companion urging him to take the medicine she was offering, but he could not take it as he was in a time lost to her.

He came to her one last time. The winter hustled in and already felt long and hard. Maria knew the date of his death, 5th December, and dreaded this last final farewell. Her school work was suffering and she spent long periods in her room with the lights out. The colours of the leaden sky cast a grim shadow and dark scars across her room.

Jenny worried about her.

"You all right, darling?" she would often say and Maria would nod, taking herself off to her room.

Maria continued to play the piano and Seb would drop whatever he was doing to go and listen at the door. There was no doubt that her reputation of being a child prodigy had been true. She was truly marvellous.

The night Mozart died, he came to her. He was pale and thin and the hair that he was so proud of lay lank against his perspiring skin. He dropped on the bed, exhausted. Maria went to the bathroom and cooled his head with a cold wet flannel and the action brought back a childhood memory. He didn't speak, but lay there silently. She took his hands and kissed them. She kissed his face delicately. She sat beside him and waited.

The next morning Jenny and Seb were woken abruptly by Mozart's 'Lacrimosa' from his Requiem being played loudly.

Jenny got out of bed and wrapped her dressing gown of vibrant pink silk around her and went to Maria's room. Maria was sat at her dressing table, her hands on her head, her hair floundering about her like a mermaid in the sea.

"Darling, darling what's up?" Jenny turned the dial on the CD player and lowered the mournful music to an acceptable level.

"He's dead, Jenny. He's dead. I'm going to miss him so much."

"Mo, Mo?" asked Jenny.

"Mo, Mo" Maria replied.

Maria stayed in her room and refused to go to school for two weeks. The 'Lacrimosa' was set at repeat but Jenny was thankful that at least it was at a level as to not to disturb her and Seb.

Patiently, Jenny took Maria trays of food which she collected again, uneaten.

One morning, to their surprise, Maria came down for breakfast saying that she was hungry and although she knew the Goldsteins were Jewish, she would like to celebrate Christmas by going shopping and buying everyone a present.

Jenny looked at Seb and Seb looked at Jenny.

"Of course, my dear," said Seb and took his wallet out to give her a hundred pounds.

Maria hesitated, but Seb commented that she could return the favour when she was rich and famous, and Maria gave him her best smile.

Chapter 20

The Royal Academy offered Maria a conditional place based on her entry exam. They also asked her to write a 1,000 word essay on a musician of her choice. Maria chose Mozart and the college was so astounded by her insight into the composer that they reduced the offer to 'unconditional' and she won her scholarship.

Over the summer, Edgar came home having finished his degree. He had secured a job at one of the many private schools in Surrey. He was impressed by the young woman presented to him and read her Royal Academy essay keenly. He had been at university for four years and in all that time had never managed to produce a piece of work like Maria's.

"She's good isn't she, mum?"

"Who, Maria? God yes, she's a bloody genius. I'm so proud that she is part of this family."

"I can see that, mum."

Jonty didn't come home for the summer, choosing to take up the offer of work in America. A friend of his father's had connections in Chicago and he was volunteering with the forensic science team for the summer months.

In September Maria left the house for her first day at the Royal Academy. Jenny had wept, something she had never done for her boys, but Maria touched her heart in a different way to them. She just seemed so vulnerable and in her own little world. She just hoped that Maria would survive.

Maria stood outside the building, marvelling at its grandeur. *I'm here at last,* she thought. She had written down the room she needed to report to and the name of the person; Janice Plant.

Maria's confidence was jolted when she found the door saying, 'Janice Plant'. She had expected to meet her on a one to one basis but other wide-eyed students were sat in a semi-circle and Janice was sat in the middle.

"Ah, you must be Maria. Come in, come in and sit next to…", she hesitated, '…erm, Jimmy." She gestured towards a Chinese man who was sat at the end of the semi-circle nearest to Maria with one seat to spare. He smiled at Maria and she noticed the creases at the side of his eyes which looked black yet jovial, and the locks of his black hair tucked in untidily behind his shirt collar.

Janice was bouncy and enthusiastic. She wore gold rimmed glasses and her clothes were a mismatch of reds and blues. Maria thought she had one of those smiles that lit up her face and she had a soothing and welcoming voice and manner.

Maria loved college life. No bells, no uniform and all the tutors were referred to by their first name. She became friends with the Chinese man, Jimmy Chu, a gifted musician and excellent sight reader. Maria spent lazy afternoons at his bedsit in Marylebone and he introduced her to jazz, which she liked. Their friendship blossomed into romance and when the couple had sex for the first time Maria was surprised to find that it hurt. She was a virgin? But what about Mozart? she puzzled.

Jimmy and Maria scoured the local second-hand shops for old records which they would play on Jimmy's vintage record player. At college they would improvise and practice the pieces from their records including Arthur Rubenstein playing the Rachmaninov Piano Concerto No.2 and Rhapsody in Blue on a theme of Paganini.

College friends became used to them as a couple and referred to them as 'the shoes' in reference to the other Jimmy Choo, which made them laugh. "I'm the patent and you're the old leather," Jimmy would joke and Maria would punch him teasingly. Secretly, Jimmy could not believe his luck. In his wildest dreams he had never imagined finding a girlfriend like Maria. He was the envy of all the men in his class and beyond. He couldn't help but notice that other men stared at her when they walked through the streets of Convent Garden or Oxford Street, or anywhere, in fact. All faces would turn when she entered a room.

The pair worked hard at college learning new pieces and practising old ones. Jimmy was a brilliant musician but not as natural as Maria. Maria could always take the music to a different level, somewhere on a different plain that was both soft and at times aggressive but whatever the piece, she would bring it back to a place that made the hairs stand up on the back of your neck.

Maria felt free for the first time. She rarely played any Mozart pieces now, as with the help of Janice and Jimmy she was introduced to a greater variety of composers. She worked out pretty quickly that she was becoming a big fan of Chopin. Beethoven had too many connotations with Mozart for her, so she avoided him, but Jimmy was a big fan and played and practised Beethoven pieces with mesmerising fixation.

She loved being alone in one of the practice rooms where she could play without disturbance from anyone. When she played she would imagine that her long fingers belonged to Chopin.

Maria invited Jimmy home for the weekend. Jenny was ecstatic and made a concerted effort to make the house tidy, warm and welcoming. She even bought some flowers from the supermarket and put them neatly in a vase on the hall table. They were the first thing that Maria noticed when she walked in.

Jenny had cooked a chicken supper and had bought a luscious chocolate desert from the patisserie. Throughout, she served deep red Australian wine. Jimmy and Seb hit it off quite nicely and talked about football. Seb ribbed Jimmy as he was a Liverpool supporter but Jimmy gave back as good as he got and Seb liked him for that.

"Would you two chaps like to have coffee in the sitting room?" asked Jenny.

"Bloody hell, Jenny, we're not Victorians, but yes, we would love to as I suspect you now want to be left alone with Maria so that you can grill her about Jimmy, heh?" He winked at Jimmy.

Maria laughed and helped Jenny clear up. Jenny did quiz her about Jimmy, but in the main she could see that she was happy.

"He seems nice."

"Yes, he is nice, Jen."

"Do you love him?"

"Yes, I think I do."

Jenny hugged her and they took the coffee and chocolate mints through to the men.

Jimmy would come and stay at the Goldstein's on alternate weekends and Jenny and Seb became accustomed to having him around. There were never any issues about where he would sleep and Jimmy shared Maria's bed. Jenny had long conversations with Maria about birth control and made an appointment for her to see the doctor who prescribed her the contraceptive pill.

Months were filled with performances, exams, theatre and film visits and walks in the park. One lazy Sunday morning Maria got out of Jimmy's bed to go to the loo and passing a chest of drawers, found a copy of 'Iron Man'.

"Iron Man," she laughed and threw it at Jimmy.

"Ouch. What's wrong with Iron Man?"

"What's right with it?" she said jokingly shouting from the behind the bathroom door.

Jimmy got up out of his slumber and pulled on his tight jeans and t-shirt and trainers. The sun poured through the Velux window and he could see turquoise sky above. His attic studio was neat and suited his needs. All the living was done in one room, including the kitchen. Maria had added some female touches and there was a vase full of bright flowers on the small table where they ate.

"I'll nip out and get some coffee and Pan au chocolat!" he shouted.

Maria shouted back, "chocolate croissants, posh boy!" and flushed the chain.

Jimmy had left before she came out so she decided to have a shower and to get dressed, then waited for Jimmy to come back.

After an hour she began to worry and then after three hours, she rang Jenny.

Jenny told Maria not to worry, he was probably distracted by a football match being played in the park, but Maria was distraught.

"Look, just as a precaution I'll ring around the hospitals just in case, just as a precaution Maria, he'll turn up, you'll see."

Jimmy had no identification on him when he was hit by the passing lorry. The hospital hadn't known who to get in touch with. All they found was a £10 note in his pocket. Someone picked up Jenny's call and said that she should come to the hospital right away as a man had been brought in fitting Jimmy's description. She rang Maria and told her to meet her there.

Maria asked the doctor if she could see Jimmy to say goodbye and Jenny insisted on going in with her. The laying-out room was sterile and bleak and Jimmy was covered in a white sheet with just his head showing.

Jenny gasped, but Maria was calm and tenderly took his hand from under the sheet and bent down to kiss it. Then she leant over and kissed his mouth.

"Goodbye Shoes," she said and nodded to Jenny that she wished to leave the room. Jenny was crying silently and her mouth was quivering as she tried to bring her tears under control. The doctor put his arm around Maria and led her out.

Two weeks later Maria was at Jimmy's flat sorting through the old records that they had collected together. The door was open and she looked up to see a young Chinese woman standing there.

"Hello," she said.

"Who are you and what are you doing in my brother's room?" asked the stranger.

"I'm Jimmy's girlfriend…was Jimmy's girlfriend."

"Oh," said the woman coming into the room. "OK, sorry, I didn't know that he had a girlfriend? Sorry," she said again.

Maria smiled. "Why are you here?"

"Just to collect his personal things. My parents would like them but please take what is yours, well, anything you want really as we won't be coming back, my parents are waiting in the funeral cortège on the way to the airport. You see, we are taking Jimmy home to cremate him."

Maria swallowed hard. "Of course, here, this box here is where he would throw in his watch and wallet and I think his passport and stuff is in the top drawer of the chest over there."

Jimmy's sister took Jimmy's things. Awkwardly, she said, "Goodbye, and thank you."

Maria just gave a small smile and watched the woman leave. Suddenly she went into panic and ran down the stairs to follow the woman who was now getting into the back of a funeral car. She saw the car carrying Jimmy's coffin behind and whispered goodbye and safe journey home to 'Shoes', sending him a tiny wave. She saw the woman and Jimmy's parents seated in the back of the car, all looking at her. She nodded at them and they nodded their heads back and then the cars drove off. She headed back upstairs to Jimmy's flat and put the old records in her bag, shut the door behind her and left for home.

Chapter 21

The college were very good, Jenny thought. They had forwarded all of Jimmy's belongings back to Hong Kong. Jimmy had made some recordings playing Beethoven pieces and Janice sent them to his parents, thinking that she could never imagine how they would feel when they heard them. She made copies and gave them to Maria.

Janice took over by keeping Maria as her ward and planned a round of concerts across London. The following year, the press had somehow managed to make the connection between this newly celebrated 20 year-old pianist with that of the young girl who had been abducted by lesbians. Jenny, Seb and Janice did what they could to protect Maria from it, and it was during this time that Henry came back into her life.

Maria had played Chopin's Nocturnes to a sell-out audience and a rousing standing ovation at Wilton's Music Hall in London, and Henry waited for her to come out of the back door.

"Hello Maria, it's Henry."

Maria looked at the man before her. There was some faint recognition.

Henry saw her puzzlement. "You know, Henry Pearson? I was your tutor when you were young, remember me? I haven't forgotten you and I have been following your success avidly. Care for a drink?"

Henry, Maria thought. The realisation of who he was dawned on her.

"Love one," she said.

Over drinks Henry related to Maria how she had learned two Mozart piano sonatas for the 'BBC Young Musician of the Year' competition but that she had to pull out last minute due to illness. During the conversation he never mentioned Magdalene and Lisa. As he spoke, memories came flooding back to Maria's mind and she found hearing someone talk to her about her childhood comforting. She arranged for Henry to call on her at Highgate where he could meet Seb and Jenny and discuss his proposals. He had changed, Maria thought, much greyer and a stoop was forming in his back, but he was still a dapper man, charming with good manners and carried with him a field of experience from the classical world.

"I hadn't thought of having an agent, Jenny, but I think I will probably need one if I am going to become a professional, and Henry has such good contacts. I've invited him over for drinks on Wednesday to meet you and Seb, is that all right?"

They were sat in the small conservatory at the back of the house, sipping tea and munching biscuits. Jenny had splashed out for a gardener and the garden had been transformed. It was landscaped to give privacy and Maria could hear birdsong coming sharp and shrill from the trimmed trees and hedges. The old summerhouse had been taken away and a new one put in its place where Jenny had secretly stocked up with her favourite wine, and she would sit there on summer evenings drinking and reading a book.

"Well I suppose that's the done thing, isn't it darling?" Jenny responded. "You knew him when you were about six or seven? How the devil did you remember him? I hope it's not going to be too painful for you?" She reached out to put her hand over Maria's, resting on the arm of the chair.

Maria squeezed her hand. "Don't worry Jen, it will be fine, you'll see, and anyway, no one could ever forget Henry - once you've met him, you'll see."

Maria and Jenny sat together quietly, watching the birds flit about, digging for worms and seeking out sour winter berries.

Henry arrived promptly at seven o'clock. Maria did not want Jenny to go to the trouble of cooking so she had bought some nibbles which she laid around the sitting room. Jenny had chilled some white wine and was already drinking a glass of red from an open bottle. Seb came in to join them. The doorbell rang and Henry was waiting with a large bunch of freesias which he gave to Maria with a smile, and kissed her on both cheeks. She invited him in and introduced him to Jenny and Seb.

"That went well," Jenny said to Seb later as Maria was seeing Henry out.

"Yes, he's a bit of a codger though. Don't you think Maria would be better off with someone younger to manage her?"

"Don't be so bloody ageist Seb, you're not far off being an old codger yourself and I'm pretty sure you wouldn't want to be put out to grass just yet."

Seb felt that Jenny said the words in a way that underpinned the unspoken fact that he had not always been quite faithful to her. However, his affair with Fiona had ended some time ago. He had seen her recently at his client's office showing off a bundle of a baby all dressed in blue, from which he gathered must have been a boy. She had looked over at him and he had half-waved not quite knowing what else to do. Life was changing and he had to admit that he was enjoying more time in the company of his wife. Maria had helped bring them together again, what with the boys grown and away from home. He guessed that Jenny would have some psycho-babble word for it, empty-nesting or some such thing he had heard her say, but no, he was happy, work was still coming in and the mortgage was all paid. He looked over at his wife who was pouring them each another glass of wine.

Seb was just about to utter something in retort when Maria came back, sat down and poured herself the end of the bottle.

"You old enough to drink?" said Seb, lifting his eyebrows in jest.

Maria laughed.

"Henry's got the first six months after my graduation all lined up. How exciting is that? There is also a concert opportunity in Prague at the Municipal Smetana Hall. I almost went there once, you know. Jenny, will you help me sort out a passport please? Henry says that you can come with me as my chaperone!"

"Jenny, a chaperone?" exclaimed Seb and they all laughed.

Jenny bought a new outfit for Maria's graduation and the boys came home to join them along with Henry.

Seb took heaps of photographs and promised to put them in a special album for her. He had considered buying Maria a car as he had done for the boys, she wasn't his daughter and he didn't feel obliged to, but he wanted to give her something as she was part of all their lives now. He discussed it with Jenny who suggested he gave her the money instead as she needed a step up. After the celebrations at the college, the family and Henry walked back to the Tube. Jenny had arranged a meal local to home so that there would be no driving involved and they could all have a drink, and she had invited Henry to stay over.

Seb took Maria to one side and gave her the envelope containing a healthy cheque. Seb looked embarrassed when Maria opened it and saw the value of the cheque. She threw her arms around him, kissed him on the cheek and thanked him profusely. Seb brushed himself down a bit and said,

"Well, you know, the boys had a car."

Jenny watched the pair and called them over to sit down as she had ordered champagne.

When it was all poured out she said, "To Maria."

Everyone chinked their glasses. "To Maria," they said.

Edgar sat next to Maria on the long imitation leather seat at one side of the dinner table, Jenny was chatting to Henry and Seb and Jonty were chatting about football.

"Congratulations Maria," he said.

"Thank you, Edgar. Thank you to you and Jonty for accepting me and putting up with me, I am so grateful, I love your mum and dad and actually I think of you and Jonty as my brothers. Jonty being the annoying one, of course!"

"Hey, I know you do. Look, stop that nonsense they're your mum and dad too, you know. Maria, I need to tell my parents something…"

Maria whispered, "Are you gay?"

"Bloody hell Maria, talk about stealing my limelight! Yes, I am and I need to tell them. How do you think they will react?"

Maria thought for a while.

"Your mother will be absolutely delighted. Can't you see her in your mind's eye telling all her friends at the book club? She'll probably write a whole piece about being a Jewish mother of a gay son in her weekly article. I guarantee she will work it in there somewhere!"

"Get that thought out of my head!" Edgar laughed.

"What thought is that?" asked Jenny, turning her attention to her eldest son.

The group seemed to hush in anticipation as Edgar replied,

"Mum, dad… I'm gay."

It seemed ages before anyone said anything then Jonty piped up,

"I knew it, I knew it, you bloody Gaylord!"

Then Jonty began to laugh and then they all began to laugh.

"Don't worry, son," said Seb. "We've known for years. Come on, it's your round." But it was Seb who went to the bar to get in more drinks and to order the food.

Jenny moved so that she could sit next to Edgar, and Maria made space for her. She could hear Jenny saying to Edgar that she had said as much to her book club group and saw Edgar's face grimacing. She winked at him and went to sit next to Henry.

Henry was bemused by Edgar's outburst. One never talked about such things during his upbringing. He had an inclination that his sister was a lesbian. He thought about Wendy, completely gaga in her nursing home. He had visited her once or twice but she didn't know who he was so he didn't go again, rather he waited for the phone call to come with the final news about the end of her life, where she would meet her God whom she had raved about so much.

He had heard that the lesbian women who had cared for Maria had been released from prison. He wondered what they were doing now.

"It's all rather marvellous Maria, family life, don't you think? Your people seem nice."

Maria was pleased that Henry referred to the Goldsteins as her people.

Chapter 22

Maria had taken a fancy to playing the violin again. She was very rusty but managed to pick out the pieces of Grieg that she remembered from her childhood. While she played she thought of 'Rose Cottage' and reflected on her life there. Jenny had told her that the two lesbian women had been released from prison. Maria inwardly resented everyone referring to them as the 'lesbians'. No one referred to Edgar as 'Gay Edgar', for God's sake. For her, those women had been mothers. They had kept her warm, fed her, nurtured her talent and had done much more than her own mother ever did. Jenny had asked her when she first came back to Highgate if she wanted to visit her mother's grave, but she had declined. Maria felt it was best to bury the thoughts of her mother inside the cold tomb that now encased her. She wasn't entirely sure either how she would feel about meeting Magdalene and Lisa again, and decided to focus on her future rather than her past.

Angie still sent cards for Maria's birthday and Maria kept in touch by sending her notelets crammed with all her news. She had called at the house after Jimmy's death and Maria was grateful. Angie was like a star to Maria, forever constant in the twilight. Maria always sent her invites to her concerts. She couldn't come to them all, of course, but did her best. She was a grandmother now to a little girl called Heavenly Boo Boo Peach. Maria thought it was a ridiculous name and this made her recall that it would be her birth name on her passport for the Prague visit, Sapphire Emerald Mortimer. That was another person all together!

Henry organised a live performance and interview on Radio 3. It was a start, he thought, to begin getting Maria's name out there. Horace Webb was jovial and enthusiastic and even plugged her next concert for her.

She played the London circuit over 4 months and Prague was looming in 5 weeks' time. Her passport had come through and Maria saw the names printed on it, names that had no possible connection with who Maria was now. Jenny was fussing, of course. She insisted that she and Maria went shopping for outfits and Maria used some of the money that Seb had given to her to buy a new evening dress for the Prague date. When she came out of the changing room Jenny was 'Wowed'!

Maria was 5' 8" and was slim built with the longest legs Jenny had ever seen. Her long hair had been cut shorter to a more sensible length and was swooped up in a version of a pony tail.

"What do you think?"

"You look amazing."

The dress had a black velvet top that scooped across the neck with one long armed sleeve. The other sleeve was absent and the dress pulled in at the waist with layers of sheer reds, crimsons and pinks.

"I can wear this for my 21st birthday," Maria said.

"It's beautiful, Maria. Right, come on, my turn, come and find me something that makes me look twenty years younger and as tall as you," Jenny said, laughing.

Meanwhile, Henry could barely control his excitement. *At last!*! he was thinking as he tied his paisley cravat in front of the mirror.

He had been up early, just as he had on that other morning and packed his bag, checked his flights on the internet and made sure his passport was in his tweed jacket. He wore chinos and a checked shirt with brown brogues. His style had not changed over the years, but he liked to dress well. He found that there was slightly more stomach to fix behind his leather belt but all in all he was pleased with the image that was staring back at him. He was meeting Maria and Jenny at the airport, and he had booked his taxi for 6am prompt. He heard the beep and looked out from his ground floor Kensington flat to see a black hackney cab outside. He gathered his things together and with his appropriate stylish leather case he got into the taxi and said, "Gatwick please."

It was with a sigh of relief that Henry saw Maria and Jenny already queuing in the Prague flight aisle. Maria saw him and waved for him to come and join them, but Henry was far too polite and joined the back of the queue. Once they had all checked in they headed for the departure lounge for breakfast.

Maria's eyes were shining. She was behaving like the little girl he remembered, fidgety and bobbing about in excitement. She was tapping her long fingers on the table as if it was a keyboard and was humming something.

"Maria's never flown before, you know, Henry. I am glad this is a short flight for her."

"I *am* here, you know!" Maria said.

Jenny shot a glance at Henry and said Maria had lived with Seb for far too long and was picking up some of his sarcasm. *Sorry,* she shrugged.

Henry seemed oblivious to Jenny and Maria as he was busy checking the monitor for the departure area.

"Ah, here we go. Gate 40."

Maria ordered wine for them all on the plane. Henry didn't want his, so Jenny drank it. As it turned out Henry was seated in the opposite aisle so he and Jenny chatted, much to the annoyance of the other passengers, for the whole journey, whilst Maria looked out from her window seat.

The take-off made Maria feel slightly nauseous but she was fascinated how quickly the plane was in the air and the green fields and winding roads disappeared from view. *The sky is so blue*, she thought. A silhouette came into her mind of a little girl wearing a white dress with a blue sash the colour of the sky tied around her waist. She could smell the whiff of a woman's pervasive scent.

When the plane had landed and the three had made their way outside to pick up a taxi to the hotel, Maria was again hopping up and down. She had her arm through Jenny's arm and Henry was carrying the cases into the back of the taxi.

The hotel was plush and very near to the concert hall where Maria would be playing the next evening. She was desperate to have a look around the old city and begged Jenny to come out with her. She agreed, but Henry decided to go to his room as he was in a need of a lie down.

"Jenny, Jenny! I love it! I love it! It's such a beautiful city!" Maria exclaimed as she and Jenny strolled along the cobbled streets and Maria let the buildings and sense of the city sink in.

Jenny could not help but be swept up in Maria's mood and the pair walked and walked until Jenny protested that she really did need to have a sit down and something to eat. They found a bistro type place across St. Charles Bridge on the old side and ordered omelettes and fries and for a change they had beer instead of wine.

Jenny was grateful for the sit down and after lunch they strolled back, passing a smart antique shop.

"Let's go and look in," Maria said.

Before she knew it Jenny found herself inside the shop. Expensive crystal chandeliers hung from the ceiling and Jenny sensed that the shop was filled with many luxurious and delicate antiquities.

Maria spotted a miniature bronze figure of a pelican bird and picked it up. Immediately the shop keeper approached her and demanded that she put it down at once. Maria eyed Jenny.

"How much is this, please?" she enquired.

The shopkeeper was gruff.

"€3,000 euro," he said with a confidence in his voice that both annoyed Jenny and Maria, for it was if to say that neither of them could afford it.

"I'll come back for it tomorrow, and I'll pay you €2,000 euro. Please see that it is wrapped and ready for Maria Amari. That's Miss Maria Amari" Maria said grandly.

She sniffed at the man, grabbed Jenny by the arm and left the shop. Maria and Jenny giggled all the way back to the hotel.

"Are you really going to buy that, Maria?"

"Yes and I'm going to get the cash out of the bank and send Henry for it. That'll teach the stuck-up man."

"That's no reason for buying it, Maria."

"I know, but I'll keep it until the day I die and it will always remind me of Prague, and of you, Jenny."

Jenny said, "Oh" as that was all she could think of to say.

Jenny and Maria met Henry for dinner at the hotel, and then they walked up to the old clock, but Maria was the only one who had the courage to walk up its tower.

Jenny left Maria to lie in bed the next morning and went down to meet Henry for breakfast. She would ask for room service to take something up for Maria later. She knew that Maria wouldn't eat before a concert as her nerves would get to her, and her tummy would make whirling noises that always made her feel embarrassed.

She chatted to Henry and probed him about the two women who had abducted Maria.

"Well, they were quite nice really you know, Jenny. Lisa was an accomplished pianist and musician in her own right but no, not a natural like Maria. I do think she had a big influence on her, though. I mean, if she had stayed with her birth mother well, she may well have died from neglect."

"She nearly did," Jenny said reminding him.

"Yes, but she would never have played the piano, you know, or any other musical instrument for that matter, if she

149

hadn't met Lisa or Magdalene. Funny, that, don't you think? There could be thousands of kids, no, millions, walking around with a gift like Maria's, never knowing it because they've never been exposed to it. Haven't you ever wondered whether Mozart would be the famous composer we now know him to be, if his father was a carpenter, for instance?"

"Don't mention Mozart to me," Jenny said.

Henry went on.

"Yes, I recall, well, it was a bit spooky you know, she had this imaginary friend called..."

Jenny interrupted Henry before he could finish what he was saying.

"Mo, Mo. Yes, I know all about Mo, Mo, but Maria's forgotten all of that now. Promise you won't mention him to Maria, Henry, promise?"

"Well, there will be a time, I'm sure that she will be asked to play some Mozart in the future."

"We'll cross that bridge when we come to it," replied Jenny.

Maria was pacing the floor at five o'clock in her hotel room. She was waiting for Jenny to come back, who had popped out to buy some painkillers for a headache. She always felt nervous before the concert and she was wishing that Jenny would hurry up so that they could get to Municipal Smetana Hall in time for her to practice the piece through. She decided to wait in the hotel lobby, and had just reached reception when Jenny arrived back.

Jenny asked the receptionist to phone Henry's room and to ask him to come down to meet them at once, sensing Maria's impatience.

Arriving at the hall, Maria loved the ambience. She had always liked Art Deco and the hall was decorated with Pre-Raphaelite style paintings in alcoves that framed arched classical pillars. When she practised on the piano the acoustics were good and she met the conductor for the first time, a Swedish man who spoke excellent English. Half an hour before the concert she went backstage and Jenny helped her to dress.

Jenny gave Maria a necklace in an art deco design and fastened it around Maria's neck. Its symmetric diamonds caught the light and Maria gave Jenny a hug.

"It's exquisite," Maria said. "Where did you get it from?"

"Ah well, you see Maria, I had no headache! I went back to that antique place and bought it. I saw it there yesterday and thought it is perfect for you! It's a gift for your 21st birthday. You're not the only one that doesn't like to be snubbed you know."

Maria giggled and threw her arms around Jenny.

"Thank you. What would I do without you?"

Jenny beamed and ushered Maria out so that they could both sneak a peek at the audience. The Prague Municipal Smetana Hall was filling up nicely and they spotted Henry sitting next to someone they both instantly recognised.

"My God," said Jenny. "That's what's his face, you know, David Soloman. I've seen him on TV."

Maria smiled to herself. *Well done, Henry,* she thought because the person sitting next to Henry was the greatest and most well-known classical publicist in the world.

The concert was a huge success and Maria played Chopin pieces that astounded her audience. There was always a quietness behind her fingers that induced a sense of calm and serenity in her playing. Maria had chosen to play Chopin's Nocturnes 1-6 and after the interval, to acknowledge her Czech audience, she played Smetana's Piano Sonata in G Minor, Op. 15. She had been lucky and practised with the violinist and cellist in the UK before travelling to Prague, so the evening went without a hitch.

Chapter 23

Maria signed across the dotted line and Henry wore a satisfied smug face like a Cheshire cat. The contract included three Chopin piano recordings, six live performances across the great capitals of Europe, and she was booked to play at the 'Last Night of the Proms.'

Maria was thrilled and excited, and her bank balance was looking promising, so she treated Henry, Jenny and Seb to a meal.

Over dinner they discussed the tour dates and the time she would need to make the recordings. Aside from this there were interviews to be held at the BBC and the broadsheets were all ringing, asking to feature Maria in their Sunday magazines. Maria didn't worry. She trusted Henry to make all the arrangements and she had agreed for him to have a 20% commission, which she felt was very generous.

Jenny checked to see whether there was a window in the schedule so that Maria could celebrate her 21st birthday. There wasn't one, so they agreed to have a small gathering at the house a few weeks afterwards.

Annabella came to the party, bringing with her a fiancée and sporting an over-sized diamond ring which she waved about when talking. Her fiancée was very good looking, and her parents, who came too, seemed relaxed and pleased with their daughter's choice of a Jewish but better still, rich husband.

Edgar brought along his new partner, Matthew, who was quiet and mousey and kind. Jonty always seemed to have a stream of girlfriends and his latest one came with him sporting a fake tan, hair extensions and bright red lipstick on her pouting mouth. Her name was Cherie.

"I bet it's not Cherie," Jenny whispered to Maria. "More likely to be Sharon!" Maria giggled in cohesion.

The evening rolled by and the buffet and pieces of birthday cake were grazed upon. Guests began to leave, until there was only Maria and Seb in the sitting room. Jenny was being gallant at trying to clear up in the kitchen, which she was much better at these days.

"Are you happy Maria? You know, with everything? You don't have to do any of this you know, if you don't want to? David Solomon will want blood you know."

Maria had kicked off her shoes and her long legs were curled at the side of her. She was drinking the remains of champagne from a crystal flute and Seb thought how elegant she looked.

"I'm really excited. In fact I can't wait. Dear old Henry has been brilliant, but between you and me, Seb, if this all goes well, I think I will have to change my agent. He is getting on a bit and the travel simply wears him out. But, I am happy for him to have his moment of glory for now. You should have seen his face in Prague. He came right onto the stage and took my arm and raised it in the air and stood and took the applause as much as if it was he who had played the Chopin Sonatas!"

"You're probably right to do that, Maria. Henry has been brilliant at bringing you to this point but sometimes things just have to change and move on. Where are you off to first? Did you say Paris?"

"Yes, Paris and then back to Prague and then Istanbul, Rome, Berlin and Austria last of all. I've arranged it with Henry so that I can have a few days in Salzburg as I want to visit the Mozart places."

Seb opened his mouth to say something and then thought better of it. *She's old enough to take care of her own life now,* he thought.

"Look, there's some more champagne in that bottle over there. Shall I grab it and bring Jenny in from the kitchen? We can have one last drink before bed."

As he moved past, Maria grabbed his arm.

"Thank you, Seb. Thank you for everything."

Seb bent down and kissed her on the head.

"You are welcome, little cherub." he said. "Mind you, you've got a lot to answer for young lady, that wife of mine has gone from Zsa Zsa Gabor to thinking she's bloody Nigella Lawson now!"

Maria laughed out loud. She stretched across the raspberry coloured sofa and stroked the cat who had come in to the room seeking warmth from the chilly night air.

"What more could a girl want?" she said to Trixie, not expecting an answer. "A man in my life, I suppose?" Maria thought of Jimmy and stroked the cat some more. She was sad to think of Jimmy cremated in a land that seemed far away and resolved that she would perform in Hong Kong one day in dedication to him. When Jenny and Seb came back she greeted them with warm smiles and raised her glass,

"To the future," she said.

Seb and Jenny raised their glasses, 'To the future," they said together.

As trusted, Henry had arranged her tour to perfection. Flights, hotels, contacts to greet them at the other end, guided tours, gym workouts and shopping trips.

Maria was well-received in every city and Henry had to handle the surge of agents and publicists and fans. Between them they crammed in as many sights as they could but the tour grew heavy on their time and Maria and Henry were resentful at not being able to visit places like the Vatican and Notre Dame, but fitted in as much as they could. In Paris

154

Maria fell in love with the area of Montmartre and Henry insisted that she have a pencil drawing done by a street artist. It was extremely good and Henry had it wrapped and sent home. He grew tired and chose to have a discussion with Maria on the eve before they flew to Salzburg.

He went to her room and poured himself a stiff whisky from the bedroom bar and she watched as he gestured with his hand if she would like one, but she shook her head. She was lying on the bed the wrong way round with her cheeks resting in her hands.

"What is it Henry? Come on, I know that look."

"Well, Maria," he said. His voice sounded hoarse. "I think after Salzburg I'm going to throw my hat in. I'm getting too old for this now, don't you think?"

He had sat next to her on the bed and she rubbed his arm.

"Oh Henry, you have been such a help to me, I'm going to miss you but we will keep in touch, won't we?"

"Always dear girl, always. Now, I've got the name of an agent from Soloman, you know, the publicist, eh? Anyway, here's her card and you are to ring her when you get back from here. She's expecting your call and she'll be the one supporting you with the recordings and interviews. Is that all right, dear?"

It was more than all right for Maria, as she had been saved from having that difficult conversation with Henry. He had unwittingly done the job for her.

Maria studied the card. It said 'Sally Field, agent for Soloman Inc.'

"It's perfectly all right, Henry. I understand, but I will miss you."

"We won't lose touch, Maria, I am your first and most loyal fan and I will be following your success avidly, dear."

Maria arrived in Salzburg with some caution, not wanting to evoke any sad memories of her hero, Mozart. She had never played any of his pieces since he left her and avoided listening to his music at all costs. That proved difficult, because she heard him everywhere. Even in supermarkets there would be a music mockery of some of his works playing over the tannoy. Her dentist even played Mozart in the waiting room.

When she arrived at her hotel, she and Henry unpacked and Henry offered to take a stroll around the streets with her. Many shop windows had chocolate or confectionery wrapped in silver foil with Mozart's profile leaping out at them. Henry thought it quite by accident, yet Maria was drawn there, when they came upon Mozart's birthplace. The house was painted a startling canary yellow in the Getreidegasse 9. It was a museum and by chance, it was open. Henry bought the tickets and Maria waited and insisted that Henry hung back from the hurrying crowd of Japanese tourists who had bought tickets just ahead of them. Maria entered the rooms. There were some of Mozart's instruments, his clavichord, his violin that he played as a child, and his harpsichord. She longed to touch them all. The rooms had been decorated tastefully in the same period. Displays held some of Mozart's documents and she read the information to herself, in German. She ambled alongside Henry, waiting to feel something. She waited for something extraordinary to happen, but nothing came to her. No revelations came to her from beyond the grave. She read the exhibitions entitled, 'A Day in the Life of a Child Prodigy'. She called to him again, but no Mozart came. Maria felt sad, as she was certain that this place would evoke something inside, but nothing stirred, just Henry who had wandered off on his own for a while and now that he had found her, said it was time to go back and prepare for the evening's concert.

The Grosses Festspielhaus wasn't as austere as she had expected. She sensed that many fabulous works of opera had been performed here. She realised that a space like this didn't have to be old to retain its spirits. It had a grand marble foyer and the lines of the festival hall's design were stately. She read a booklet which said that this was the original place of the royal stables, which made her laugh a little. *All those dames and grand dames*, she thought, *reaching climatic singing heights on the surface of where horses used to poo and wee.*

She liked the feel of this place and looked forward to the concert. She was having her nails manicured and chose a bright red polish to match the silk of her new dress. Her tummy was rumbling and the manicurist looked up at her, alarmed.

Henry had organised this last evening of her tour to have a quick turnaround, guessing that Maria would not want to prolong her stay in Austria. Tonight her programme consisted of Chopin's

PolonaiseNo.1 in C sharp minor, Op.26

PolonaiseNo.2 in E flat minor, Op.26

Polonaise No.3 in A, Op.40 No.1 'Military'

PolonaiseNo.4 in C minor, Op.40 PolonaiseNo.5 in F sharp minor, Op.44

PolonaiseNo.6 in A flat, and Op.53 'Heroic'

Polonaise No.7 in A flat, Op.61 'Polonaise-Fantasie'.

Henry had factored in an interval and then afterwards it was straight back to the airport to fly home. Jenny had called Henry's mobile to check the flight times as she was going to be waiting for them at the airport.

Once again the applause for Maria was resounding. She bowed gracefully and a boy dressed in a suit of corn blue came on stage and gave her a monumentally sized bouquet of flowers. He could barely carry it on, and one of the stage hands came to help him. The audience tittered. Maria could see a sea of hands rippling and bowed again. She took hold of the little boy's hand and led him off stage. Four curtain calls later and feeling exhausted, Henry guided her to the waiting taxi and they sped off to the airport.

When she woke the next morning, Jenny had prepared a breakfast tray which she had left on the chest of drawers. She had picked some flowers from the garden and put them in a spotty jug and the tray was laid with tea and milk in a matching spotty china cup and saucer. There was a boiled egg with soldier bread and warm buttery brioche. Maria sat up and pulled the tray onto her lap.

She looked around the room. Her boy band poster was still on the wall, and there was a collage of her and Annabella dressed up as St. Trinian's girls at the school dance. She had placed her bronze pelican on the mantel over the painted white fireplace. A butterfly flitted in through the window and landed on the white duvet, its peacock colours bright and bold. *I wonder if that's a sign of something?* she thought.

Maria felt as if a new dawn was occurring in her life. When she got up, she searched for the card in her handbag that Henry had given to her. She flipped it across her hand.

"Come on then, Sally," she said. "Let's see what you can do for me, shall we?"

Maria arranged a small dinner party for Henry, to thank him for his years of devotion, and she gave him a pair of gold cufflinks engraved with his initials, as well as a card. He accepted them gracefully and kissed Maria on both cheeks. Sighing, he said,

"If only I was 20 years younger."

Maria viewed him. Dear old Henry. He was beginning to look his age now, approaching 70 perhaps, and yet his eyes still burned blue and he had the vigour and strength of a man much younger. She threw her arms around him.

"If I was only 50 years older," she said to comfort him, but it didn't sound right at all and Jenny and Seb laughed.

"We know what you mean, darling," Jenny said.

After the weekend Maria dialled Sally's mobile phone number. She had already left Sally a message and was a bit perturbed that Sally hadn't got back to her already.

She heard the posh tones of a woman at the other end who sounded like she smoked rather a lot. Her voice was coarse.

"Sally Field, here."

Sally arranged to meet with Maria at a pub in Greenwich which was near to where she lived. When Maria walked into the pub she spotted Sally straight away. Her dyed blonde hair was tied up in a chignon and she wore an expensive looking cashmere sweater in green which picked out the colours of her eyes, and a camel coloured pencil skirt with fishnet tights and high heeled black shoes. Maria put her age at around 40 although this might be rather flattering to Sally, as when Maria got closer to her she noticed that she was plastered in make-up. Maria's instincts had been right, this woman was a smoker and she smelled it on her when Sally beckoned for her to sit next to her.

Sally extended her a hand to shake, and Maria took it.

Sally was very inquisitive about Maria, where she lived how often she practiced and so on.

"We simply must get you out of that Highgate House. How old are you now? 22, 23? No matter, you really should have a place of your own by now, you know. You must be earning enough?"

Maria let Sally chatter on but inside she realised that Sally was right, it was time for her to have her own place and some independence. It was like Henry's departure was the end of an era.

The lunch was rather boozy and when Maria headed back to the train station she ran into the newsagents to grab a bottle of water. There were some free local housing magazines for Greenwich so she picked one up to read on the train back.

Chapter 24

The next year was an extremely busy one for Maria. Not only did she make three CD recordings but she was booked for the Last Night of the Proms. For a change and to the astonishment of everyone, she chose to play Rachmaninov's Piano Concerto No. 2 in C Minor Op. 18. Everything about this composition reminded her of Jimmy. Most of it was new to her, but she was determined to learn it. She and Jimmy had really only mucked about and improvised with the piece.

During this time, Maria put in an offer on a terraced house in one of the back streets of Greenwich. Her offer was accepted and Maria found herself owning a home of her own for the first time. She liked Greenwich, people seemed friendly and it was very convenient for all amenities. Jenny helped her to pick out the decor and fabrics and soon the house was warm and cosy. There was no room for a piano but this did not matter as the music studio had made an offer for her to practise there at a minimal monthly rent.

She had found a dressmaker to make her a dress out of Union Jack material. Underneath was a shorter version and the Velcro could be stripped back to reveal it. All of this was done in secret and no one knew apart from her and the conductor who was lead at the Prom. He had got her number from Sally and he had telephoned to pass the idea by her.

"I think people will find it hugely funny and I'll have the orchestra play along."

Maria was up for some fun and agreed that she would sing a duet with an up and coming young jazz musician, André Pascal, who had a wide female fan base, before she went on to play the Rachmaninov. She would arrive in her over dress and he would rip it off to reveal the shorter one beneath as part of their act.

The BBC had also called Sally to see if Maria would be happy to record her 'Desert Island Discs'.

This caused a problem for Maria as she had to narrow her choices down to eight. Just for a laugh she snuck in an old version of the jazz duet, not wanting to give any clues away but realising that people would put two and two together after the Prom.

She took off to the recording studio and was surprised when the interviewer asked her about Lisa and Magdalene. Had no one told her that she did not wish to discuss them? Embarrassed, the presenter passed over the question and rapidly asked Maria for her next song. She chose Ralph Sutton playing 'Love Lies' because it was a song that she and Jimmy had listened to together.

The presenter said, "And I hear that you are actually going to Hong Kong next year to perform, Maria? Is that right?"

Maria corrected the interviewer and told her how excited she was at the prospect of going in three months' time and how she was really looking forward to it. It was rare for a British performer to play there, she had told the interviewer, and the whole night's performance was going to be dedicated to Jimmy. She added that she was delighted to be working with Jan Van Dyke, the guest conductor at the Proms, who had pulled it all together for her.

"It was a now or never thing," she told the interviewer. "The calendar is usually fixed a year in advance so I am very lucky to be going. I am so excited to have another opportunity to be directed by the great Jan van Dyke in Hong Kong."

The proms night was a huge success and her Union Jack costume had caused rapturous applause and laughter. People blew their horns and shot balloons across the air. It was the most fun she had ever had at a concert and resolved that she would tell Sally that she would love to do it again. It was like stepping into what seemed like a bullring where she could reach out to the audience. It was a wonderful experience.

Jan van Dyke was a magnificent conductor and director. There was an aura about him which she recognised. Like her, he seamlessly brought the notes together and he had been a child prodigy, playing the violin to critical acclaim around the world. He specialised in Vivaldi and she considered whether when he was a young bright boy, the red-haired, bearded - and by all accounts womanising - composer had visited him. She felt sure that he had.

Maria's career was reaching its zenith. Wherever she played she received brilliant reviews and whatever she played the dates would be sold out well in advance of the concert dates.

Sally had filled Henry's shoes admirably and all the preparations were underway for her trip to Hong Kong. Sally had booked her a suite in a hotel. "You can afford it now, darling," she said out of the corner of her mouth into the phone as she puffed on a cigarette, with the smoke rising up to stain her dyed blonde hair with a streak of yellow. Maria didn't feel like a prima donna and didn't want to be treated like one either. The thought of a suite felt diva-ish but as it was only for two nights, why not?

A taxi came trundling up the cobbled street to Maria's house and the cabbie leapt out and rang the bell.

"Ave to be quick darlin' as I'm double-parked owt here."

The taxi driver needn't have worried as Maria was all packed and ready to go.

She felt lonely travelling on her own as she had been used to Jenny or Henry being about. The journey was long and arduous as Maria's long legs felt cramped in the window seat she was assigned. She still enjoyed the views from the plane window and as it came to land in Hong Kong all she could make out was an ocean of multi-colours in the evening light.

Good to her word, Sally had a taxi waiting and a Chinese man was holding a card with her name in arrivals, and he whisked Maria off to the hotel.

This time she had decided to play some of the Chopin Etudes. More difficult, she knew, but she sensed the audience would be more discerning in their critiques than those in Europe. She based her decision on Jimmy's high standards and sensed that the Chinese seemed to have an air of perfect expectations.

At the hotel there was a party of people waiting to greet her. She hardly caught any of their names as they all seemed to be talking at her at once, and she was grateful when a smartly dressed girl in the uniform of the hotel called over the luggage boy and firmly led her through the crowd to the lift.

Maria smiled at the girl and she smiled back and said in faltering English,

"You are celebrity?"

Maria wasn't sure how to respond but smiled wider and was pleased when the lift door opened and the girl showed her to her suite. She was wrestling in her mind whether she should tip the girl or the luggage boy but decided both, and they both said something in Mandarin to her which she did not understand but smiled gladly back at them.

The suite was like a royal palace. There was a large living area with gold gilded chairs in lavender and cream stripes with pastel cerise printed wallpaper, ornate with glowing exotic birds. In the bedroom was the biggest bed she had ever seen and then when she visited the bathroom she swore out loud that it was the biggest bath tub she had ever seen.

"Ooooh, I could get used to this," she said to no one.

She ran a deep bath using the fragrant hotel bubble bath which whizzed up into a bursting froth and smelled of jasmine. The floor was under-heated and the towels were deep and soft. Maria had poured herself a glass of wine and placed it on the shelf made for just such a thing and stepped into the bath. She put her hands in front of her face and stroked off the bubbles to look at her long fingers tipped with crimson nail varnish on her medium length fingernails. Lately she had been listening to Eric Sate, and she listened to his gentleness as she popped in her iPhone ear plugs, balancing the phone on the shelf with the wine. The softness of the music made her think of Jimmy and she let a tear cascade down her cheek. She sipped the wine and toasted 'Shoes'. "For you," she said.

She looked down at her hands that he had once held.

"Bless these hands and thank you to whom ever made them for me. I am truly grateful." Maria was thinking deeply and an image of her mother came into her head. She sighed and swept those past thoughts from her mind and focused on tomorrow.

The receptionist rang in the morning to inform her that two gentlemen in respect of the concert were waiting in reception for her. She was already dressed in tan straight slacks, black pump shoes and a smart white blouse. She had tied a purple scarf with butterflies fashionably around her neck, and tied her hair into a neat bun.

In the lobby she saw her picture gracing the front of magazines and newspapers. No wonder the girl had thought she was a celebrity.

At the desk she met Mr Chinn and Mr Brigstock, both from the company who had organised the night's performance. They escorted her out to their plush car and ordered the driver to take them to the City Hall Concert Hall.

Maria had also decided to include the Rachmaninov as it was still fresh in her brain, and she luckily had time before leaving London to rehearse with Jan Van Dyke again - the Hong Kong Musical Director and Chief conductor who had been to the UK as special guest conductor for the Last Night of the Proms. Maria thought him a genius. Jan's musical ability was undoubted. He had conducted some of the greatest orchestras in the world.

His Dutch accent was both soothing yet determined and she liked his style. He had worked very hard, on her behalf, for her to perform in Hong Kong, but he had great influence and without causing too much inconvenience to anyone Jan had fixed the date for one night. "It's now or never," he had said, and Maria had accepted his offer, gladly fulfilling her promise to Jimmy.

Jan Van dyke interested her greatly. During rehearsal breaks they discussed Mozart's genius and Maria dared to mention that she had always thought that Mozart was probably on the autistic spectrum. She was pleased to hear that Jan agreed, having an autistic child himself. Maria found it odd talking so deeply about Mozart, but he had left her long ago, and she was unperturbed by their frank discussions. Frustratingly, there was no time to discuss things with Jan at any length as time was of the essence. Jan pushed Maria and the Hong Kong Philharmonic Orchestra to their limits and they continued on until the late afternoon, until Jan was satisfied that they could break for a few hours. He informed Maria that she would have time to rest before that night's performance, for which she was relieved.

Jan studied Maria. She was beautiful and her eyes were deep, and, he thought, full of hidden mystery. It was a risk leaving the rehearsal so late before the concert but he had no doubt of Maria's ability or of his own orchestra, who had played all the pieces many times. *Maria is like a Goddess,* he thought. *She is gifted, talented and beautiful. I hope she realises how blessed she is?*

The Hong Kong audiences were dynamic in their response to Maria's concert performance. Afterwards some of the orchestra, Jan, Mr Chinn and Mr Brigstock headed back to the bar at Maria's hotel. The girl from the hotel gave Maria an envelope which she slipped into her bag to read later. For now, she wallowed in her own success and she praised Jan and the orchestra members with mutual admiration.

Maria was tired and went up to her room, leaving members of the orchestra, who were becoming louder from the intake of alcohol, with a bottle of champagne she ordered from the bar. It was the nice girl who served her and Maria wondered whether she ever got any rest. The girl handed her a white napkin and asked Maria for her autograph in broken English. Maria signed with a flourish and the girl grinned and bowed her head.

The South China Morning Post acclaimed her a 'living Goddess' and reading the article she saw that they had quoted Jan. He had kissed her on the cheek goodbye last evening and all he had said was, "We will work together again, Maria" as he took her hands into his. He bent to kiss them. "Beautiful hands, Maria. You must care for them. Yes?"

The British Sunday broadsheets had an article about Maria Amari which Jenny was reading at the kitchen table.

"Look Seb, it says here that Maria has been asked to act in a film about Mozart. She's not said anything to you, has she?"

Seb took the paper. "It says here that it is a fresh look at Mozart, directed by some Australian bloke. I wonder if she'll do it? Can Maria act?"

Jenny cast her eyes over the paper. "That girl can do whatever she wants, but Mozart? Do you think she's ready for this, Seb?"

Seb didn't answer her question, and instead said,

"I see the Hong Kong concert was a huge hit. Only Maria could pull that off at such short notice."

"Yes, I told you she would," replied Jenny.

Meanwhile, Maria was on the long flight home. She fished in her bag for a tissue and found the envelope that the hotel girl had handed to her. She had forgotten about it. It had her name on the front delicately written in italics in old-fashioned black ink. She opened it.

Dear Miss Amari,

I understand that you have come to Hong Kong to play here in my brother's memory.

Please understand that our family would like to thank you. It is an honour to us.

Yours,

Tina Chu.

It was a short letter but its meaning meant much. Maria's eyes grew steamy. She placed the letter back in its envelope and held it in her hand for the rest of the journey.

Chapter 25

On arriving home Maria felt jet-lagged and went for a lie down. The phone rang. It was Jenny.

"Maria darling, how are you?"

Maria could not get a word in edgeways as Jenny rabbited on about some film and Hong Kong and could they meet for lunch tomorrow? Jenny would travel over to Greenwich and suggested meeting at Maria's local pub.

Maria found Jenny, seated. She had already ordered Thai fishcakes for them both. Her brown hair was tied in a bright scarlet scarf with blue and yellow swirls and she had a Bohemian look about her in her flowing skirt and jangly bangles.

Maria smiled, pleased to see a friendly face. Over lunch they chatted and Jenny told her about the article in the Sunday newspaper about the new film. Maria said she didn't know anything about it but she was due to meet with Sally tomorrow and would interrogate her, suspecting it was some publicity stunt that Sally had created. After lunch Jenny held Maria, kissing her profusely and telling her 'How proud we all are of you darling'. "All the papers are raving about you. Hong Kong was a huge success by all accounts. Clever girl!" Then she said as an afterthought, "By the way, Oh my God, I can't believe I haven't told you, Jonty's getting married next summer! No, Maria, not to the fake tan girl, a nice Jewish girl he met in the states. An all-American wedding, her father's in the government or something or another, anyway the wedding is in Washington. Perhaps you could play something for them? I'll ring with the dates. I hope you are not working, we all want you to be there, Maria."

Maria laughed at Jenny who was speaking so fast she had to sit down for a minute before she left.

"Of course I'll be there. I wouldn't miss it for the world!"

Maria was intrigued by the mention of the new Mozart film. She had seen some of the films the director had made before and she had loved their edge and sharpness, together with the overall feeling of things that were never said within the films, yet were brought to the surface with subtlety and uniqueness. She wondered whether she could act. She had been in the school play as one of the 'Three Little Maids' but that was about it.

As soon as she got back home she rang Sally. Sally said that she would reveal all tomorrow and agreed to meet with Maria in the same pub she'd had lunch with Jenny.

It was a Saturday and that afternoon England had played and won a rugby match against Ireland. The pub was filled with men and women wearing rugby shirts and every now and again opposing supporters burst into song together. The atmosphere was convivial and noisy. Maria saw Sally, who had managed to grab the same place where she had lunch with Jenny. The table was tucked neatly in a bay window and the sun was shining through on the boisterous crowd. The women greeted each other by air kisses on both cheeks. Maria had gotten used to Sally's form of hello and Sally had never made contact on Maria's cheeks, so Maria often wondered why she bothered with this salutation at all.

Settling down in the evening sun that cast speckled shadows through the bay, Sally brought Maria up to date with all her news about the film. It was the studio who had leaked the news to the press, but Sally had been in long conversations with the Director who was absolutely resolute that it was she, Maria, whom he wanted to play Nannerl (Anna Maria was her real name, but everyone called her Nannerl), Mozart's sister. It sounded exciting and Maria was keen to find out more. Sally had arranged a meeting next week at a smart London restaurant with the Director and Producer of the film and Sally was going along too, as her agent, of course.

The deal was agreed and Maria found her diary for the next three months was going to be filled with acting and singing lessons, and for the next six months after that she would be filming on location across Europe. The film excited her more than she could believe and she enjoyed the lessons and being with the other cast members. Everyone was friendly and kind and helpful, coaxing the shyness out of her so that soon the drama coach swore that he could teach Maria no more. Maria had to sing in the film and her voice coach, a vibrant woman in her thirties, belied her own talent by concentrating and giving so much to Maria that Maria brought her small gifts each time she had a lesson, out of appreciation. She too had an autistic child and this fascinated Maria, who shared her Mozart theory.

"Maybe you can bring in some of those emotions to the part of Nannerl?" her voice coach suggested. "Perhaps Nannerl was more empathetic towards the young Mozart because she suspected the boy had difficulties? There is a dark side somewhere there Maria, try and pull this out in your acting."

Maria mentioned it to the Director who thought it was a great idea. In the heat of the summer, the filming began.

Maria found the days long as often filming would start at the crack of dawn and not finish until late at night. She found the long periods of waiting tedious and arranged for an electronic keyboard to be put in her mobile dressing room so that she could at least keep up some minimal practice.

The actor playing Mozart as a grown man was handsome and Maria advised on how his hair should be and the way that the composer held himself. She had an inclination that he rather fancied her, but her feelings were not reciprocal as she suspected that he likely had affairs with all his leading ladies. She certainly thought he was sneaking into the dressing room of the actress who was playing his wife, Constanze.

Maria tried hard to imagine how the film would play in her head but the scenes were so out of order that she found the whole thing hard to follow.

Both the director and producer were precious over the rushes and the editing of the film was done in secret, and no one was allowed to see the end result until opening night.

Maria had finished all her parts by the time Christmas arrived and she chose to indulge herself in a bit of retail therapy. One cold winter's morning she caught the train to Knightsbridge and hit the big department stores, purchasing gifts for the Goldsteins, Angie, Henry and Sally. She saw a distinguished fountain pen in a shagreen case and asked for it to be wrapped and sent to Jan Van Dyke.

It was whilst shopping that two black men approached her. They were looking at her oddly as if she was a creature from the deep, someone who was barely recognisable to them. She assumed they must be fans. One of the men spoke.

"Are you Maria?" he asked.

"Yes, I am," she replied. "Can I help you?"

"Well, you won't remember us but it was us who saved you the day you fell. We rang the ambulance and well, my brother and I have followed your success ever since. We've got all your CDs."

The other brother spoke, seeing the shock on Maria's face.

"Sorry, we didn't mean to frighten or upset you. We just wanted to say, 'hello'."

Maria composed herself.

"Of course, of course, lovely to meet you." She shook both their hands but the moment was awkward. She faltered, "Thank you for doing that, you know, ringing the ambulance."

"Well, good luck," said the first brother. "Bye."

"Thank you. Goodbye both," she replied.

Maria had a strange sense of her past creeping upon her. It was hot in the store and she headed quickly for the exit, longing to reach home.

Later that evening she was meeting up with Sally for drinks. She hadn't seen Sally for most of the summer whilst she had been busy filming, and she looked forward to a catch up.

Her usual pub was busy with Christmas revellers and people grabbing a quick drink before home. Sally was sat in their usual seat under the bay window which was decked with fairy lights and plastic holly wreaths. Sally greeted Maria with 'air kisses' and Maria sat beside her, facing out towards the swelling crowd.

The pair chatted eagerly about the film and Maria gave Sally an autograph from the leading man. Sally was thrilled as he was a bit of a 'pin up' to her. Maria went to the bar to order some more drinks and as she stood at the bar she noticed a man standing on the corner at the other side, also waiting to be served. There was something familiar about him which she could not quite work out. He looked over at her and smiled. She noticed some realisation hit his face.

"My God! Maria, Maria, is that you?" The man jostled through the crowd to reach her, ducking under beams as he approached her.

Maria wore an expression of concern. Was this man a fan, and was he going to be bothersome?

"Maria, Maria, it's me Freddie, and look, look over there, there's Peter!"

Maria looked to where the man was pointing and saw a man seated next to an appealing girl who looked identical to the man who was now accosting her. The only difference was that the man in front of her had a broken nose. She looked at what he was wearing, casual jeans and a rugby shirt and guessed his disjointed nose was a casualty of a rugby match. He was broad and his smile showed white even teeth.

Freddie watched as the realisation and recognition dawned on Maria's face.

"Oh my God, Freddie! Freddie from Kent? How lovely to see you."

Freddie awkwardly put his arms around her to hug her.

"Yes, Maria, do you remember me now?"

Maria nodded silently and looked across at Peter. Memories hurtled back in her mind and she was a child again in a big garden, climbing trees with her knees scraped.

"Little Maria, God you used to boss us two about something wicked," he said.

At that moment the barman appeared and asked Maria for her order.

"I am sorry but I am here with a friend, well, my agent actually, I'll have to get back to her."

Freddie smiled. He took a beer mat from the bar and scrawled his mobile phone number across it and gave it to her, sticking it between her clutched fingers.

"Ring me," he said.

"I will," Maria replied and held the two glasses of wine high above her head as she mingled her way back to Sally.

"Hmmm, who was that charming fellow?" asked Sally.

"An old friend," said Maria.

"You must introduce him darling, next time?"

Maria drank her wine gazing over heads to search him out but he must have gone to sit back with his brother, as she couldn't see him.

"Yes, next time," she said.

Maria spent Christmas with the Goldsteins and Jenny cooked a large chicken for lunch. Edgar came with Matthew and announced that they would be getting married as soon as the new law was passed to allow it. It would be a quiet affair at the registry office, unlike his brother's, whose wedding was turning out to be quite something and probably costing a huge amount. Jenny was beside herself with glee at the news. Everyone was surprised that she was taking the news so well as there would be nothing Jewish about the ceremony, but all guessed that Jonty's wedding would make up for anything that

Edgar's lacked. She caught Maria's eye as she was digging in to a roast potato.

"It will be Maria next!"

Maria smiled. "Not for a while, there's no one special. You know, not since Jimmy."

She knew she had brought the tone of the dinner to a low and brightened up by saying that when she did, she wanted Seb to give her away and everyone chinked their glasses at that and Seb just muttered to himself, 'Oh Lord.'

It was that time after Christmas, before the New Year, when everyone is exhausted from shopping, cooking and over-eating and yet looking forward to seeing the New Year in.

Maria arrived back at Greenwich and saw the beer mat on the coffee table where she had thrown it down.

She picked it up and managed to work out the numbers of Freddie's phone and dialled.

"Hello, Freddie speaking..."

Peter and his wife were throwing a drinks party for the New Year and then people were going on to one of the local hotels for midnight celebrations. As it turned out, both Freddie and Peter lived in Greenwich. Peter had been married for a few years and his wife had recently given birth to twins, a boy and a girl called Eva and Max. Peter's wife, Mary, looked tired and carried a baby monitor clipped to her hip as she poured drinks and offered canapés to her guests. Maria learned that Peter and Mary had met at university and had been inseparable ever since.

Maria looked exceptionally beautiful this evening, dressed in a short black dress with an open back, showing off the curves of her spine, and she wore high heels which she was pleased to see still made her shorter than Freddie.

Freddie was dressed in dark jeans and a smart jacket, shirt and tie, and he had brought a gift of perfume for Maria which she sprayed all over her neck and put in her clutch bag. It was fragrant and smelled of Jasmine, momentarily reminding her of her trip to Hong Kong and the huge bath tub.

Peter was telling his wife all about Maria, and Maria was nodding politely and interjected now and again as they reflected on childhood memories. Peter recalled how Maria would order Freddie and Peter to dress up as nurses so that she could be the doctor and order them about a bit.

"We really missed you, Maria."

Maria sighed. "Well, just because we're all grown up doesn't mean that I still can't do a bit of ordering about! Now Peter, may I have another drink please?"

Peter obliged and Maria and Mary laughed together at his obedience.

Maria felt a warmness towards Peter and Mary, and she accepted their invitation for lunch next Sunday so that she could meet the 'twins'.

Freddie was engaged in conversation with one of Peter's work colleagues, who Maria gleaned worked in the 'City' as they all appeared to be doing, including Freddie.

Freddie edged his way towards Maria and pulled her away into a corner of the sitting room. The room had originally been two, the same design as Maria's house, but had been knocked into one. It was homely with modern original watercolours hanging on the walls, and an open fireplace mantel held numerous photographs of Peter, Mary and the twins and linked families.

"How are your parents?" Maria asked, noticing a picture of what must have been Helen and Tony holding their new twin grandchildren quite proudly.

"They had another set of twins, you know. Girls this time, called Edith and Florence. We call them Eddie and Flo. To be honest they were definitely not planned but mum loves having girls around and dad simply dotes on them. Sixteen now, and horse bloody mad. We hardly ever see them as they are always riding or moonstruck in a stable. It seems they are pretty good at all that horsey stuff as they have been selected for the British Junior Equestrian Team." He was shouting over the music and the hum of the party.

"Shall we head off for the hotel and have a drink there, where we can talk?"

Maria agreed and grabbed her wrap which Freddie gallantly helped to fold around her. Then he put his arm around her which was firm and comforting. Maria didn't mind the gesture and leaned in towards his body as they meandered their way across the cobbled streets towards the hotel.

After the midnight balloon popping and a few drunken renditions of 'Auld Lang Syne' Freddie and Maria stayed up, until the early morning light seeped through the heavy curtains to seek the couple out together on a signature hotel sofa.

Freddie told Maria that he had been engaged and the bride had even bought the dress. "We paid for the venue, flowers, cars, everything", he told her, but a week before the wedding she had called the whole thing off and informed him by text that she was seeing his best friend Rob and had been for quite some time. Freddie had been devastated and told Maria how he had taken a mate with him on the honeymoon instead.

"A week in the Seychelles with a farting, sweating mate was not so much fun", he said, "but my mate got me through the difficult times," he said with a devilish grin on his face.

He was holding Maria's hand and took her chin in the other one, and kissed her. It was the sexiest kiss she had ever known and she responded with passion. His mouth was warm and she felt safe in his arms. The couple lay on the hotel sofa and Maria talked about her life and she felt sure that a new romance was dawning.

Freddie walked her home and said that he would see her at Peter's for lunch. He stopped at her door and kissed her again and Maria longed for him to come in, but sensed that this was best left until another time.

Maria took some flowers and a good bottle of wine to Peter and Mary, who greeted her warmly at the door. Freddie greeted her with a kiss and Mary served a delicious lunch. The conversation was light and the twins were cute and cuddly. Whilst Peter and Mary cleared the table she and Freddie sat on the floor with the twins, playing with their toys and having fun. Peter and Mary watched and wondered whether this was going to be a scene from the future.

Chapter 26

Freddie and Maria's romance developed. Jenny was happy, and Sally was envious.

At the opening night of the film, 'Mozart the Man', Maria asked Freddie to join her and he agreed, despite Maria's warnings of the circus it would be. "The press will pick up that you are with me," she told him.

"I'd better make sure that I give them my best side then," he had sniggered.

The film opening was a glamorous affair with lots of famous actors, some flying in from America and Australia. A large crowd had gathered in Leicester Square, waiting patiently to glimpse the stars of the film, and they snapped away on their mobile phones and called out actor's names to turn this way and that, stretching themselves across the barriers. Maria wore a gold coloured dress with an evocative split between her breasts. A large jewellery house bedecked her with diamonds, emeralds and pearls on loan for the evening. The press photographers were greedy as they snapped away, believing Maria to be an enchantress as she beguiled them with her natural beauty. Freddie did not let his impatience show and mixed happily with cast and crew, sharing jokes and marvelling at his girlfriend who held all who spoke to her in her spell.

Returning late in the early hours of the morning Maria did not need to ask Freddie in. He began to kiss her on the step and as she opened the door he began to undress her. Jimmy's love-making had been tentative and soft. Freddie was urgent and passionate and she knew that every part of his body desired her.

Maria was in love with Freddie. She loved his familiarity and when he asked her to marry him, she jumped into his arms for joy. They agreed to set the date for a couple of years ahead as both Jonty and Edgar were getting married soon, and Maria selfishly wanted all the focus to be on her and Freddie on their wedding day, and she wanted time to plan.

Freddie worked long hours in the City, so sold his flat and moved in with Maria so the pair could see more of each other. Maria released a recording of the songs from the film. She was also approached by a well-known Rhythm and Blues man to sing duets with him. Both albums got into the top 10 download and regular music charts. She saw herself in shop windows that advertised her new album with the croaky crooner, Jonny Frank, dressed in a white jacket and tie. The cover of the CD only showed the singers from the waist up and Maria was slightly alarmed at how much of her cleavage was showing in her sea-green strapless dress, and how the crooner seemed to be focused on her breasts. She hadn't noticed that before, but assumed it was a tactic to help sell the albums. It still astonished her to see her own image reflected back.

Freddie invited Maria to meet Helen and Tony. He drove down to Kent and they passed, 'Rose Cottage.' It looked the same as she remembered and Freddie had taken her hand as they drove past and squeezed it reassuringly.

Helen and Tony were delighted to meet with Maria, and after an excellent lunch suggested a walk. Freddie had his arm around Maria as they strolled along. Eddie and Flo had gone off to the stables and Helen and Tony ambled behind, pointing out the church where they stopped for a while to admire the stained glass windows.

"Do you ever see the lesbian women?" Tony enquired.

Helen dug him in the ribs.

Maria turned to him, smiling, and confessed that she never had. Although people from her past seemed to be popping up like jack-in-the-boxes recently, she had said, smiling at Freddie.

Helen suggested that they head back for coffee and chastised Tony all the way back for his remark, which amused everyone.

To the relief of the sponsors, the film, 'Mozart the Man' was a box office hit. People were beginning to recognise Maria more and more and she sometimes found this irritating, especially when she was out with Freddie.

Soon after the opening night, Maria telephoned Freddie.

"Hi darling. A very glamorous envelope arrived this morning and I have been nominated as 'Best supporting Actress' at the British Film Academy Awards. . Will you go with me?" she asked Freddie, tentatively.

"Darling, that's wonderful news, of course I will!" replied Freddie, much to Maria's relief.

The theatre was packed with Hollywood stars and Maria and Freddie found themselves sitting next to an American married couple who had courted a lot of publicity over the years, but each was a brilliant actor and Maria and Freddie liked them both as they chatted and laughed together at the awards ceremony and the after show party.

Maria wore a sheer purple halter neck and was genuinely surprised when her name was called out as winner of the prize. Freddie kissed her and the American couple stood up and kissed her as she stepped past them on her way to the stage.

Maria loved the attention and despite not having a speech ready, she did a good job of thanking all the people involved in the making of the film and the director shouted out her name and cheered. The after show party went on until the late morning sun rose above the London skyline. Freddie enjoyed the event and once again received admiring looks from the males in the room for bagging the desirable Maria. Maria however, was completely ignorant of the male attention in the room and this was one of the reasons why Freddie loved her so.

One day in the warming light of the early summer that followed, Maria was coming out of her house on her way to a meeting with Sally when she was stopped by a woman. She was short and plump and had wild dark hair with an involuntary grey track that shot down the middle. She had big brown eyes and when she spoke, Maria detected an Irish accent.

"Maria, it's Magdalene. Do you remember me?"

Maria's head swam. She felt faint and sick and her nerves were on edge as she took in the woman in front of her. At first she thought it was a fan who had tracked her down. This thought annoyed her, as she thought her Greenwich home was becoming less safe from pesky fans. Then her thoughts coordinated with the realisation that it was Magdalene.

She was unsteady, and Magdalene reached out to hold her but Maria pulled her arm away.

"What do you want?" Maria asked sharply.

"I just wanted to see you were all right, that's all. Maria, Lisa and I have thought about you every day and what we did. But we loved you, Maria. We still love you and we saved you from certain death."

Magdalene reprimanded herself for the last bit, as it came out in a different way than how she'd meant to say it.

Maria surveyed her.

"I don't want to talk to you. Please go away and leave me alone."

Magdalene looked crestfallen.

"I only want to talk to you Maria. Just to explain. I don't live in Kent now, Lisa and I live in Wales, Llangollen. I don't have much time before my train goes back. If you could just spare me five minutes, Maria, it would mean a lot to me."

Maria looked at her watch.

"Five minutes, that's all. There's a tea room on the way to the station, let's go there."

Magdalene got the tea and sat down. Maria noticed how the fat on her chin wobbled as she took off her coat and scarf from around her creased and crumpled neck.

Maria listened patiently as Magdalene brushed over the prison time and spoke about how she had seen her at the door on that day of her interview all those years ago, and knew that she could not leave her behind. The five minutes rolled into an hour and Magdalene answered Maria's questions openly. Maria rang Sally to apologise that she would have to put the office meeting off until tomorrow as she had been delayed, but she didn't explain why.

At the end of their meeting Maria found that she had agreed to visit Magdalene and Lisa at their home in Wales. She could not grasp why, but felt that the women deserved some of her time. Maria admitted that there was something about her recollection of Lisa that she liked and she had also warmed to Magdalene enough to organise the trip to Wales the following month.

When Maria relayed what had happened to Freddie he was surprised, but promised to drive her.

Maria and Freddie set off to Llangollen and on the way Freddie told her about two women who lived together over 100 years ago and were lovers, known as 'The Ladies of Llangollen.'

Maria was impressed by his knowledge, to which he confessed he only knew because he had searched on the internet to find where Llangollen was and it had come up.

Via a solicitor, Magdalene had sold the cottage in Kent whilst she was in prison and made a substantial profit, so that she and Lisa could purchase the neat faux black and white house at the brow of a hill on the outskirts of Llangollen.

Maria felt apprehensive as Freddie pulled into the drive. She saw curtains flinch and guessed at the anticipation that her visit would bring.

Magdalene opened the door and welcomed her and Freddie in. The hall was filled with pictures of Maria, like a shrine, cut-outs from newspapers and magazines embellished the walls. Freddie felt it was a bit sinister and was glad that he came. They were led into the sitting room of the small detached house where Lisa was sitting on the edge of a winged-back chair. The room was decorated from another period. Victorian style dark furniture was arranged around a marble fireplace with a gas fire, and the decor was fussy and garish. Maria noticed the upright piano, where silver antique frames with pictures of Maria as a child were arranged. Lisa was wearing a neat printed floral dress with a yellow cardigan tied at her slim waist. Her natural blonde hair was swept into a ponytail and her heavy framed glasses sat above a small mouth coated in pale pink lipstick. Maria absorbed the smells, the hues of the room and the hairs on the back of her neck rose up, pricking at her senses.

Lisa seemed not to know whether to shake hands or hug Maria and hesitated at the formality. Maria offered her own hand and felt Lisa's thin hand, her fingers long like hers.

Magdalene went to make tea and Freddie asked for the bathroom.

Lisa looked over at Maria.

"It's so lovely to see you after all this time. You have grown into a stunning woman Maria, your photographs don't do you justice."

Lisa wore an expression of someone who has suffered, and Maria wondered how Lisa had handled prison. She looked fragile and there was desolation in her eyes.

Magdalene came in with a tea tray and Freddie returned from the bathroom, and with a glance at Maria, asked where he could buy petrol for the homeward journey. Magdalene walked to the car with him to show him directions. All the women knew that he was being discreet, leaving them together to talk about things in the past.

Left alone, Lisa took the photos from the piano top and before long there was laughter as the two lovers related stories to Maria. They discussed Maria's proneness to be precocious as a child and her ability to have her own way in all things. Mo, Mo was not mentioned and any reference to Mozart was skirted by as Lisa and Magdalene understood that some things were better left unsaid.

Magdalene produced an album where she and Lisa had pasted in stories and photographs about Maria, their tickets for the showing of the Mozart film and other bits and bobs related to Maria. Maria sat in the middle of the two *new* ladies of Llangollen scanning the albums and Freddie returned. Lisa made more tea and loaded the tray with triangular sandwiches and cake which Freddie devoured.

"And you, Freddie. Look at you! My, how you have grown and changed too, but I think we still recognise that mischievous face," Magdalene said.

Lisa joined in,

"Fate is a funny thing isn't it. You know, you two meeting and getting engaged."

Freddie looked at his watch.

"Well yes," he replied. "Sorry, Maria, we must go, darling before it gets too late."

Maria stood up to go and as she was leaving she turned to Lisa and Magdalene.

"I'd love for you to come to our wedding. You are right after all; fate does have a funny way of dealing with things. Thank you, thank you, Magdalene and Lisa. Say you will come, won't you?"

The two women exchanged happy looks and shouted back, "Yes, yes we'll come, let us know when... goodbye Maria, goodbye."

Maria waved from the car window and Freddie tooted the horn.

"All right, my love, Maria? How was it? Are you OK?"

"It was fine, Freddie. Gosh, I've got a lot of planning to do for our wedding, but don't think you are going to get off that easy, Freddie Chad. We need to sort out a venue and you are coming with me."

Edgar's wedding was a small affair as he said it would be. His partner Matthew's parents didn't come along as they didn't approve of their son being gay, so Jenny, in her usual fashion, made an extra effort by saying that she was his mum now and not to worry because she didn't mind that he was in love with her son at all. She was digging at the luncheon afterwards to see whether Edgar and Matthew had any plans to adopt, as she was desperate to be a grandma and Maria and Freddie smirked, watching Edgar and his partner cringe. Seb was leaning at the bar with Annabella's parents. Jonty wasn't there as he and his bride to be were knee deep in the final arrangements of their own wedding.

"Are we going to make Jenny a grandparent?" Freddie looked at Maria.

"It will be fun practising," he added.

"Wait and see, Freddie, I haven't thought about it. Actually, have you?"

"Not 'til now. But I guess we should? That's if you want to?"

"Straight away. Let's not leave it too late. Let's try after the wedding, Freddie"

Freddie smiled at his gorgeous fiancée and snogged her in full view of the guests, until Seb came and poked him in the back.

Jonty's wedding was everything that Jenny had hoped for. Big and lavish and expensive. The ceremony was held in the garden at the bride's parents' house and Freddie made comments to Maria about the size of the bride's bottom, which she tried to ignore but he set her giggling all the same. Afterwards the 200 plus guests were ushered into a marquee.

"Do you know, this marquee is huge but it has had made no impact on reducing the size of this lawn at all." Jenny was remarking to no one in particular as they sat down to the wedding breakfast.

It turned out that the bride's father was a democratic senator and a close friend of the President who unfortunately, because of more pressing political engagements, could not attend but he had made a special video of his good wishes to the bride and groom, which impressed Jenny no end and was something she could not wait to tell the book club group all about. In fact she was busily tapping into her mobile phone with the news when Seb snatched it from her and told her to pay attention as the speeches were just about to start. Jenny pouted and grabbed her phone and put it in her bag. She moaned that she could not hear what people were saying and Seb had to keep telling her to sshhh.

At last it was time for the wedding party and guests to relax, and later on in the evening more people arrived who Jenny said were 'very important', and the band played all night long. Maria played a small jazz piece and sang 'Summer Time', mostly at the insistence of Jenny.

"I don't think your arse will look as big as hers," Freddie said teasingly to Maria as she was undressing for bed. Freddie was already in it with both hands behind his head. Maria looked at his strong arms, his muscles defined.

"Don't be mean, it was just the style of the dress, that's all."

She jumped into bed and gave Freddie a friendly slap.

He took her in his arms and made love to her. Afterwards, he held her tightly.

"I can't wait for our wedding day, Maria" and then he made a noise like an evil laugh, 'Mwhahahha! You will be mine, mine, all mine!"

Chapter 27

Jenny, as it turned out, was less of a hindrance in helping Maria with her wedding plans than she thought she was going to be. Whilst Freddie was in the City she and Jenny took trips out to the countryside until Maria settled on the venue for her wedding and took Freddie at the weekend for his opinion.

Jenny created a 'mood board' and Maria chose a peach theme. Not strong peach colours, but delicate. She was having her dress made by a well-known designer who was making it for free in exchange for the publicity. Jenny organised all the flowers, from the wedding bouquets down to the table centres.

Freddie had taken Seb out for a drink and asked him if he could marry Maria. It was something Maria wanted as she considered Seb to be her father. It didn't quite happen as formally as she had expected as she heard from Jenny later that she had to put Freddie to bed as he was in no fit state to go home, and that both men had frightful headaches in the morning. She rang Maria and left a message so she wouldn't worry. That evening sparked a bond between Freddie and Seb and the two could be often found in cohorts, chatting about football or rugby matches or finding any excuse to slope off to the pub. Neither Maria nor Jenny minded as their attentions were focused on the big day.

Jenny thought that Maria had been rather candid about her visit to Llangollen but she had noticed that Maria seemed more content than she had ever seen her.

Maria spoke to Jenny about having a child and confessed that she had postponed all her performances for a year after the wedding. Jenny was delighted and rushed off to buy paint and paper for Maria's old room, to turn in it into a nursery. Jenny knew that Edgar would have no children and if Jonty did, she knew she probably wouldn't get a look in, so all her hopes were pinned on Maria.

At last the wedding day dawned. The sky was kind and azure blue with flighty clouds. Freddie stayed over at Peter's and Jenny slept in the spare room at Maria's so she could help her prepare for her big day.

The press had got hold of the story and were hanging about outside. Jenny, opening her curtains and seeing the melee, opened the window and shouted, 'Bugger Off!' The reporters and photographers took no notice and were still there when the time came for Maria to leave the house.

A shiny black Phantom was waiting for her, to sweep her off to the venue. At Peter's she had arranged the same for Freddie. Peter's twins were adorable, dressed in peach as token pageboy and bridesmaid and were seated next to 'Uncle Freddie' as their car sped off.

As Maria left, cameras flashed and journalists shouted for her to 'look this way and this' and Jenny pushed them aside, guiding Maria to the car.

Her dress was simple. It was in a delicate ivory silk in a bias cut which showed Maria's gorgeous figure and emphasised her long legs. The top was shaped into a sweetheart cut and she wore a flimsy sheer wrap across her shoulders. She was wearing the necklace that Jenny had bought for her and on the eve of their wedding Freddie gave her some diamond earrings that without further inspection looked to match the necklace. Maria wore her hair up with pretty peach flowers fixed in a neat row across the crown of her head.

Jenny wore a peach coloured suit and a cream hat with peach plumed feathers. She had difficulty walking through doors as it was so large. *There's no mistaking the mother of the bride*, Maria thought.

When the car drove into the long drive, reaching up to the creaking old hall, Maria took in a deep breath.

Jenny helped her out of the car, ensuring that her dress didn't snag, and Maria saw Seb waiting to greet her.

"Hello, my dear," he said. "You look beautiful, nay, beyond beauty. There's a very nervous groom waiting for you in there, lucky man."

Maria took his arm and walked past the chairs filled with family and friends. Sally was doing her best to smile and Jenny was getting in the way of the photographer as he pointed his camera at Maria.

Maria saw Magdalene and Lisa. They had come, and for a moment her mind went back to a vision of white and cerulean. Then she saw Freddie.

After the ceremony, the lunch was exquisite and the speeches hilarious. Seb's speech had the crowd bursting with his humour and more poignantly he spoke of beautiful and talented Maria, and how blessed that he and his wife had been to come to know her. Peter was best man and stuttered through his speech but still made everyone laugh and his sisters, for once, were out of their jodhpurs, ungainly dressed in the peach bridesmaid dresses that Maria had picked out for them.

Maria had arranged the seating plan so that Sally and Henry sat together and she noticed that the two were being quite intimate. "Still life in the old boy yet," she thought.

Freddie's speech was romantic and some of the female guests were tearful, not from sadness but from joy at his outspoken love for Maria.

Maria and Freddie danced the night away and the evening was full of frolics and fun. The couple were ecstatic in their love for one another and it shone through.

A glossy magazine had rights to their wedding photographs and Freddie was slightly angry when Maria suggested this to him. When she told him how much money they would pay the couple, he quickly changed his mind agreeing that the sum would be helpful in the future so throughout the day they stopped and allowed guests and friends to be photographed and interviewed. Jenny bought ten copies of the magazine, keeping two for Freddie and Maria for when they returned from their honeymoon. Jenny was over the moon as she peered at herself, looking for all the world like a film star in her over-sized hat.

Freddie and Maria honeymooned in the South of France, choosing to hire a villa with a pool. They spent lazy days swimming and reading and ventured out occasionally for an evening meal or a trip to a vineyard. They frequently made love and often shared baths and showers together.

Two weeks sped by and they returned to Greenwich, where everything was the same. The streets around the Cutty Sark were full of tourists and when Freddie returned to work Maria decided that it was a time for a move.

She found an old house in Kent, commutable for Freddie, not far from the village where she had once lived and not too far away from her new in-laws, as secretly she was hoping that Helen and Tony would be perfect babysitters for the child she was carrying inside her.

It was a Georgian House with spacious rooms and high ceilings. It was similar to her in-laws' house, but she liked the order of the rooms and the way the house flowed. There was room for a grand piano in the drawing room and she treated herself to an antique with a tone that suited her and one she felt at one with. It was expensive but she didn't care. She looked down at her fingers when she played it and said a hushed thank you. Freddie would not dream of Maria decorating, so within a few weeks the decorators had done their work, new furniture was bought and the house became a home.

After three months she registered with the local doctor, a nice man called Doctor Wainwright. He examined Maria by taking her blood pressure and asked her to do a 'wee' for him, which she obliged into a test tube. He took out a horn shaped device and rested it on Maria's tummy, making hmmmm sounds.

Maria and her baby were well.

Maria cooked a romantic meal and lit candles on the dinner table. She put on a smooth CD on the Hi-Fi and made up her face, shaping her bewitching almond eyes with black Kohl.

Freddie arrived home to his new house, where Maria sat him down and announced her news to him. Freddie jumped about, swinging his wife in his arms, kissing her frantically calling her, 'his clever girl.' When he set her down she said,

"I take it you're pleased then?"

Freddie was an attentive husband. He would dash home from work as early as he could. He arranged for the return of the decorators and Maria spent pleasant afternoons choosing the scheme for the nursery and selected a soothing lemon colour. This left Maria time to practice on her new piano with her baby growing inside her. Dr Wainwright told her that she could pay a sum of money to find out the sex of the baby but Maria had declined, as she wanted a surprise.

Jenny was like a mothering hen, constantly on the telephone or popping in for a cup of tea.

"You can't just pop in here all the way from Highgate for a cup of tea!" Freddie would say, but Maria accepted Jenny's visits and was glad to see her.

As her time grew near, her bulk made her uncomfortable and she bought a maternity pillow which she could wrap around her. She barely slept and felt her voice grow raspy from sheer tiredness.

Maria woke Freddie in the night. The bed was soaked, her waters had broken.

Sophie Maria Chad was born at 08.05am, the morning after the night that Maria had gone into labour. Maria could not describe the pain and she had lashed out at Freddie calling him a 'bastard to do this to me' before the doctor came to give her an epidural.

Sophie weighed 9 lbs and 6oz. She was pink and bonnie and Maria and Freddie cooed and cooed over their precious little girl. The hospital where she was born was new, and the nurses were bemused by the press who came to take pictures of the new addition to their ward, but they could spot the reporters a mile off and did a good job of warding them away.

When Maria returned home Freddie had filled the house with flowers. The nursery was fresh and he had placed the Moses basket by their bed until Sophie was old enough to move into her own room.

Days and weeks went by. Sally nagged Maria about getting back to work but Maria was enjoying being a mother to Sophie.

When Freddie had to work late in his 'busy period' Maria would drive over to stay with Jenny and Seb. Jenny had decorated Maria's old room in cheerful dusky pinks and one day, when Maria was putting Sophie down for an afternoon nap, a butterfly fluttered in and rested on the cot. *Perhaps it is a sign*? she thought. *But of what?*

Jonty visited and it was nice to see him and his wife. No sign of a baby yet, Jenny had alluded to Maria.

"Give them time," Maria had said. Sadly, Jonty revealed to his mother a year later that his wife could not have children. They had seen the best specialists and had all the tests but to no avail. His wife was visibly upset and Jonty had to break the news to his mother gently during one of their summer vacations to the UK. These trips included a visit home for a week, and the rest of the time Jonty and his wife motored around Scotland or Wales, or took a flight to Ireland or Paris. Jonty's father-in-law had secured Jonty a job and he and his wife Juliette had set up a home together where they enjoyed each other's company and Juliette kept a bountiful garden in Washington.

Jenny seemed to accept this news stoically, but this made her more attentive towards Maria and Sophie.

Freddie was loving and caring towards his wife and lavished his time equally between her and his daughter. His pace at work was slowing and he managed to get home earlier in the evenings to spend more time with Sophie before she went to bed. He marvelled at his growing child, as there was no doubting she was bright and talented. Helen and Tony would babysit when Freddie and Maria wanted to go out for a meal or take a trip up to London to see a show, concert, or to see friends.

Since the awards ceremonies, they had been visited by the American couple they had met who had two girls of similar age to Sophie. Kelly and Braden told amusing stories about celebrity cosmetic surgery and the Americans enjoyed having friends in the English countryside. Freddie and Maria liked their down-to-earth company and were grateful for that, as they would eat casseroles and have long walks in the countryside together as the children played and rolled down grassy banks.

There was an open invitation for reciprocal visits and Maria and Freddie planned to fly to the States once Sophie had finished her first school year.

Magdalene and Lisa also visited Maria and Sophie and brought old photographs of Maria with them so they could all compare likenesses.

As Sophie grew, it was evident that her father's genes were the strongest. Helen told Maria that Freddie and Peter both had fair hair and blue eyes as babies, and Sophie was just like them.

"You got away from having twins but next time, Maria, be careful!" Helen warned repeatedly but Maria wasn't planning on having any more children.

When Sophie was a toddler she would sit on Maria's knee whilst she played on her grand piano. Sophie would squeal and bash the notes with her closed fists. *At least her fingers are long like mine,* Maria would think as she stroked her hand through Sophie's blond curls.

As she grew, Sophie's talking skills were exceptional and Magdalene and Lisa had said that Maria was just the same at that age. Sophie was working out numbers in her head and she could pick out simple nursery tunes on the piano. Recently, she was pestering Maria to teach her how to play more advanced tunes and Maria had succumbed, teaching Sophie 'Twinkle, Twinkle Little Star.' Sophie picked it up straight away so Maria showed her how to play the notes with her left hand and Sophie learned to play the tune with both hands within an hour of Maria showing her. Maria began to teach Sophie how to read music. Her little girl took the sheets to the kitchen table, took a crayon and began to copy out her own notes which she would then take back to the piano and play the tune proudly to her admiring mother.

Life was good for the Chads but Maria longed to perform again. Over dinner one evening, Maria broached the subject of returning to work with Freddie. A gigantic cosmetic group had contacted her as they wanted to use her hands to model a range of nail varnish. However, when she had turned up for the shoot they were so amazed by her looks that they signed her up for a three year contract to model make-up as well. Maria enjoyed the modelling and the pay was good, but her love was her music and she longed to get back to playing to live audiences. Freddie saw the look in his wife's eyes and understood.

Maria rang Sally to ask her to start making some in-roads into her comeback, and Sally was delighted to renew their professional relationship. "I'll be ready to come back when Sophie goes to school in a few months..."

Maria put down the phone, pleased that her plans were going well.

Chapter 28

Maria was in a happy mood, singing and humming, as she had received a contract from the recording company. They had included an invitation for an awards ceremony and hinted that her album with crooner Jonny Frank was up for an award as best-selling album in that category. She guessed that Freddie would not want to go because of work demands, so she had called Sally to ask if she would accompany her and Sally was beside herself with glee.

At times Maria was bored, and filled her time when she was not looking after Sophie by reading or composing or practising new scores on the piano. She was learning some Sate pieces and his music calmed her.

This day, she'd prepared lunch for Sophie and was loading the dishwasher, her slim fingers daintily placing the dishes in neat rows. Her fingernails were polished, glinting from her last cosmetic shoot and she gazed at them. Her thoughts, just lately, were on her strange return to her past in Kent and she began to think deeply about her life and her gift. She looked down at her hands. *I wonder if I am on the autistic spectrum?* she thought. *I can't explain how I know how to play the piano. I can't explain how I know notes that follow each other, I just do. It always seems like the composer is in my head, spiritually guiding me. If I can't explain it then goodness knows, no one else can.*

She was daydreaming and looking forward to getting back to her profession. She loved caring full-time for Sophie, but the time was right for her to start her career again. Helen and Jenny would always be on hand to babysit and she would plan things so she would never be away from home for more than two nights. She looked around her ordered kitchen and wondered whether her obsession with tidiness was normal.

At that moment a butterfly flitted through the window and rested on the counter top, its bright colours sheen and glossy. Maria stared at it long and hard.

Sophie had been jabbering, but Maria had not been listening.

She went to sit next to Sophie at the oak wood table in her designer kitchen. Sophie was nearing five and completely ready for school. She sat dipping her spoon in and out of the bananas and custard that Maria had prepared for dessert.

Maria got up to clear the table and she passed the counter top, but the butterfly had gone. She looked around for it but she could see it nowhere.

The sunshine left the window and a gloomy shadow reached inwardly to where she stood. A feeling of dread poked at her bones and darkness swirled in her eyes. She turned back to look at Sophie.

She was abruptly shaken as she heard Sophie say very loudly and excitedly,

"Look mummy, LOOK!", then,

"Mo, Mo's here!"

Maria froze and looked where Sophie was pointing. The dish left her hand and fell to the ground, breaking into splinters, and the leftover custard splashed like yellow paint drops across the polished floor.

The End